James O'Halloran

A Christmas Truce Carol

CURRACH
PRESS

First edition, 2012, published by
CURRACH PRESS
55A Spruce Avenue, Stillorgan Industrial Park,
Blackrock, County Dublin

Cover by Bill Bolger
Cover picture by Maurice Pierse
Origination by The Columba Press
Printed by MPG Books

ISBN 978 1 85607 790 3

Acknowledgements

Jennifer Armstrong (ed.), Sean Connolly, Don Mullan (the novel found its inspiration in Don's Christmas Truce Project, which in turn resulted from his relationship with the late Fr Sean McFerran SDB), Steve Harris, Michael Corcoran Jnr, Paddy Hogan, my Family, Val Collier, Salesian companions and friends, Amanda Moreno (Royal Irish Fusiliers Museum, Armagh), Jonathan Maguire (Royal Irish Fusiliers Museum, Armagh), Andy Edwards (sculptor), Pete Cheilens (Flanders Field Museum), Sandy Evrard (Mayor of Mesen/Messines), Patrick Florissoone (Mesen Town Secretary), Steven Reynaert (Culture Director), Philip Delmotte (Mesen/Messines Peace Village), Roland Roseel (Mesen/Messines Peace Village), Andre (Guide: 'Flanders Over the Top Tours'), Stefaan Vanmoereke, (President emeritus, 'De Vredesduif' – 'The Peace Pigeon'), Eric Talavet, Privates James Burke, Thomas Rochford, and Michael Corcoran (soldiers in the Great War) for their captivating stories. For all the veterans of the Great War who were neighbours of the writer in Scaugh, Callan, Co. Kilkenny. In the course of his research, the author read widely (non-fiction, fiction, diaries) on the First World War generally and on the Christmas Truce in particular and is indebted to a whole plethora of writers. However, he would like to make special mention of Malcolm Brown and Shirley Seaton's *Christmas Truce*, one of the key works on the subject.

So here, while the mad guns curse overhead,
And tired men sigh with mud for couch and floor,
Know that we fools, now with the foolish dead,
Died not for flag, nor King, nor Emperor,
But for a dream, born in a herdsman's shed,
And for the secret Scripture of the poor.
(To My Daughter Betty, T. M. Kettle)

From behind the lines came voices crying, 'English soldiers, English soldiers, Happy Christmas. Where are your Christmas trees?' and faint but clear, the songs of the season. We were a little embarrassed by this comradeship and, as a lasting joke against us, let it be said that the order was given to stand to arms. But we did not fire, for the battalion on our right, the Royal Irish Rifles, with their national sense of humour, answered the enemy's salutations with songs and jokes and made appointments in No Man's Land for Christmas Day.
(Regimental History of the 13/London Regiment)

STAVE ONE

The Dogs of War

It was December 1914 and young Private Michael Cochrane was standing guard in a bleak Flanders' trench. Nearby, squatting in slime, was his pal Lenny Barton incinerating lice in the seams of his clothes with a glowing cigarette tip. The legs of both men were swathed mummy-like in bandages to protect their raw trench feet. They were a long way from their hometown of Ballybeg in the Irish county of Kilkenny.

Michael was being eagerly regarded by a malignant, beady-eyed rat. The outsized tawny creature that had battened on the flesh of his dead comrades was well camouflaged against the yellowish soil of the trench. These vermin were known to have brazenly attacked even cats and dogs in a manner that turned nature on its head. But then, the whole world seemed dark and out of joint at that time.

Michael first saw the rat as it sprang at him and sank its razor-sharp teeth unerringly into his throat. The young soldier screamed, dropping the crude periscope through which he had been observing the German trenches opposite. In a total panic, he grabbed the beast and strove to drag it away, but he was only tearing the throat out of himself. Barton ran to his side, crying out to others for help. Immediately half a dozen comrades squelched to the scene from various parts of the dog-toothed trench.

'What'll we do?' yelled Barton.

Sergeant Clinch didn't speak. He simply knocked Michael out with the butt of his rifle, bayoneted the rat and prised its teeth apart. He then slung the vermin as far as he could into No Man's Land.

As Cochrane lay unconscious in the muddy trench, a young, fresh-faced officer barked an order to the company runner: 'Moore, go and get the RAMC chaps to come and attend to this lad.' Everyone had confidence in Brian Moore, an old sweat who had been with 2nd Battalion of the Royal Dublin Fusiliers since the Boer War and had landed in France just as the present conflict broke out. The Dublin Fusiliers were of course an Irish regiment. Though many of its men were from Co. Dublin, others came from neighbouring counties such as Kildare, Wicklow, Carlow, Kilkenny and elsewhere. Some were even from parts of England. The role of runner was a perilous one in the current industrialised slaughter, but if anyone could keep himself alive it would be the experienced Moore.

'Lieutenant Leveridge, sir, what assessment will I give of Private Cochrane's condition?'

'Could be serious. We don't know. Just hurry.'

'Yes, sir.'

The incongruity of being called 'sir' by a man much older and more experienced than himself didn't seem to dawn on Leveridge. The class system was alive and well, even among the horrors of the front, and commissioned officers, however young, were regarded as a cut above the lower ranks. It was just how things were. And to be fair to them, in general they acquitted themselves well, were considerate towards their men and fearless in battle.

Leveridge had recently replaced Captain Cyril McGuinness, who was killed in a foray on the German lines near Ploegsteert Wood, or 'Plugstreet Wood' as the Tommies called it. In that foray, the Dubliners captured some yards of ground with severe losses. McGuinness valiantly urged on his men while he himself was armed only with a swagger stick, as was the custom for some officers in the early days of this holocaust. And holocaust it was, with more than 50,000 casualties suffered by the British Expeditionary Force already. Killing on a scale never witnessed before. It was scheduled to be over by Christmas. But, as one facetious Tommy remarked, 'They didn't say what Christmas!' A piece of shrapnel through the head in the shape of a minute cannon ball had ended the young life of Captain McGuinness. The precious yards gained under McGuinness were recaptured by the Germans the following day.

As Moore sped off, other comrades remained with the profusely bleeding Michael Cochrane. They tried to staunch the flow by wrapping a linen cloth around his neck. Besides Leveridge, who hailed from England's Hampshire, and Barton from Kilkenny (as was indeed Cochrane), there was Sergeant Christopher Clinch, a Dubliner like Moore and also a veteran of the Boer War, Private Sean Furlong from Carlow and Private George Belford who hailed from Kildare. This group constituted half of a section pertaining to 'B' Company, 2/Royal Dublin Fusiliers. The other half was pinned down in another part of the trench by concentrated artillery fire. And there was the persistent rat-tat-tat of a machine-gun that had claimed the lives of five Dubliners in recent days.

Surveying the fraught scene, Leveridge remarked, 'You boys have had no shortage of drama since getting to France in August.'

Among other disasters, did he have in mind that he was their third Commanding Officer? First there was the Boer War veteran Captain Byrne, blown to pieces at the Marne, and then McGuinness killed in his early twenties. Casualties now meant that young leaders were replacing the regulars who began the war.

In reply Barton said, 'You're right, sir, we've had plenty of fireworks. Took quite a roasting during the long arduous retreat from Mons.'

'Would you tell me about it?'

'It was a nightmare. Lots of men taken prisoner.'

'That must have been tough on morale.'

'Devastating. We gave as good as we got, but took a battering that left us badly depleted at Le Cateau, the Aisne and Armentières. Severed heads and limbs were a daily spectacle, men spilling their guts in the mud and drowning in it if they fell off the duckboards, and, everywhere, blood. God it was terrible. I don't want to be haunted by it, though I know I will be for the rest of my life. Now I know there is a hell. I've been there. There was one incident in particular — '

'Yes? Please go on.'

'I saw a poor fellow with half of his handsome face sliced away by shrapnel at Le Cateau – good looks on one side and a grinning exposed skeleton on the other. Before anyone could stop the whimpering casualty, he recklessly jumped out of the dugout and shot at the enemy, but was instantly felled by sniper fire.'

'What possessed him to do that?'

'Maybe it was intentional … It's too painful to talk about it, sir. Unless you were there, you couldn't possibly understand the depths of the horror.'

'I'm sure you're right, Barton.'

'Eventually the war bogged down on the Aisne.'

There was silence after Barton spoke. Leveridge, who had only joined the Dubliners in Belgium, was now a wiser man. Despite the horror of what he had heard, he had a foreboding that there was worse to come, but he kept that to himself. 'And now we're mired in the treacly mud of Flanders,' he mused.

'Being destroyed by General Mud,' added the tall, rangy Clinch.

'And what attracted you to this war, Barton?' asked Leveridge.

'It may surprise you to hear, sir, that I came in search of a bride.'

'A bride!' The officer was indeed perplexed.

'Listen, pal,' interrupted Sean Furlong, 'I think you'll be disappointed. I've searched all the trenches for miles around and the only bit of skirt I have seen was among the Scottish Seaforth Highlanders! I doubt if those hairy legged specimens would fit the bill.'

This tickled the group. A quiet smile momentarily appeared even on the strained face of Cochrane, who was regaining consciousness.

Barton turned towards Leveridge. Again the officer was surprised. Barton's face had grown grave and a tear dimmed his eye. 'It's a long story. If you want, I will tell you sometime. And what brought you here, sir?'

'Oh, I was in my final year at Oxford. There was great excitement there. None of us wanted to miss this show. The fear was that it would be over before we got here. We had no idea what it would be like. Many of my fellow students are already dead and the rest are mired down.'

Four medics arrived with Moore and did some preliminary work on Cochrane. They cleaned up and disinfected the wound, applied some iodine and put on temporary bandaging. They then laid him on a stretcher and took him away to a dressing station. Mortars were still doing their worst so they had to crouch as they hurried along through the somewhat shallow communication trenches.

Before leaving, Cochrane had whispered to Barton, 'Lenny, don't mention anything about this if you write home. I hope it's nothing serious and I don't want to get the family worried.'

'Okay, Michael. But you could be lucky enough to get a furlough and a chance to see your family. In that case tell my own people that I am fine and thinking of them. And on the quiet would you ever give my love to Eileen Walsh and give her this,' he handed him a lovely medal of the Virgin Mary. 'The Chaplain, Fr Ryan, gave it to me, but I have a cross, a gift from Eileen.'

'You know something, Lenny? You're not a bad ould Protestant at all, at all,' said Cochrane feebly and squeezed his hand.

As he watched them go, Clinch noted, 'Amazing how much better constructed the German trenches are towards ours,' – he had managed to see one during a foray into enemy territory. 'They are deep, have wicker-work sides and duckboard bottoms above channels designed to take away the water. They even have stone blockhouses warmed by stoves. When there is a lull in the fighting, the men can slip in there, rest and give their clothes a chance to dry out. I tell you, it's the Ritz by comparison with our shabby set-up.'

'Trouble is,' noted Leveridge, 'that people in command like French, Haig, Smith-Dorrien and others think only in terms of horses and glorious charges of the Light Brigade. Punch holes in the German defences and let in the horses, they'll do the business. Hapless animals against machine-guns. Fatuous! Those dino - saurs don't realise that this is a dig-in war, a war of attrition. The Germans do though. They intend to grind us down until we beg for a settlement. Different strategies. If we don't break through, the victory will be theirs.'

'Well,' said Moore, 'the sooner this war of contrition is over and we can all go home the better.'

'It's "attrition", Moorie.' Furlong corrected him.

'Didn't I say "contrition"?' answered a puzzled Moore.

'Yes, that's what you said.'

Before Furlong could explain, Leveridge tried to restore some order. 'Men, it's time to get back to your stations. A command has come through from Company HQ to put that murderous Gerry machine-gun out of commission. I'm to send a group out after dark to deal with it. I've chosen you, Clinch, together with Barton and Private Frank Gill from that group further down the trench.'

'I can see why you'd choose a Boer War vet like Clinch,' said Barton. 'But why me?'

'You were picked because you are teacher's pet,' the mischievous Furlong chipped in.

'Lucky me,' added Barton wryly.

'You may not have been in the Boer War, but you got to the army a bit before the others and you have been involved in the present action from the start. I'll trust you to look after yourself,' said Leveridge. 'Now get some bully and Maconochie's stew into you –'

'Yummy, yummy,' interrupted Furlong.

'And get some rest.' If you didn't have the chirpy Furlong in this outfit, you'd have to invent him, thought the Lieutenant.

'As a matter of interest, sir, why Frank Gill?' enquired Barton.

'He's a recently arrived Kitchener volunteer.'

'True, but in civvy street he was a keen potholer and must have done a lot of crawling in his day. That skill will be crucial tonight.'

'Quite a few generals have made good use of it on their way up the ranks.'

'Behave yourself, Furlong, or I'll send you instead.' Furlong's mouth snapped shut.

***

Fortunately, that night was overcast. Just after dark Clinch, Barton and Gill began the long crawl to the offending machine-gun post. If they stood upright and a flare went up, they could be cut down by sniper-fire.

They soon melted into the darkness. The plan was to get around to the rear of the gun and surprise the operators. Gingerly they headed for their objective; inch by inch they approached.

Now and again, a flare would light up No Man's Land and in those fraught moments they would flatten themselves even more on the ground and hold their breath in terror. Occasionally, too, a shell would explode – one close enough to shower them with debris. The flares and shells were to discourage escapades such as theirs.

At one point, Clinch felt he heard a faint voice nearby. Possibly a German cadre out on some mission of its own. Anxiously, they lay doggo for a long time to allow any such group to distance itself.

After what seemed an eon they got behind the machine-gun post. They could hear the occupants speaking. They could practically hear them breathe. At that moment a flare with a red hue to it soared skywards. It became as bright as day. They hugged the ground. So muddied had they become that they were indistinguishable from the surrounding landscape. The three closed their eyes and waited with bated breath. Nothing happened. The Germans were scanning the land in front of them, but didn't look behind. Then one gave a half-glance backward as the flare fizzled out. Did he spot them? No gunfire followed. It seemed he didn't.

They backtracked somewhat so that they could communicate with each other.

'That red flare looked like one that would be used at a carnival or something,' whispered Gill.

'The fireworks are coming now,' said Clinch. 'Are you all set?'

'Yes.'

'This has to be a knife job. I'll take the big fellow in the middle. Gill, you get the one on the right. Barton, the one on the left is yours. I'll give a hand signal for the attack.'

They crawled nearer once more. Clinch gave the signal.

They pounced on the three men. Placing a hand over his mouth, Barton plunged a knife into his man's back. With lightning speed, Clinch cut the big fellow's throat. But Gill's man was not unprepared. His rifle was close by. Barton grabbed him as he was about to fire and deflected the bullet, while Clinch despatched the gunman. Gill groaned in agony, otherwise the post was silenced.

'How bad is it?' Clinch asked Gill.

'It's my leg, Sergeant.'

'Can you crawl?'

'Not as I've always done,' he replied wryly. 'I'll give it a go though. I'm sorry about what happened, Sergeant.'

'Nothing to be sorry for. You played your part.'

Having destroyed the machine-gun, they needed to leave quickly. Barton paused and looked at the three prone figures. 'This will mean heartbreak for three German families.'

'No time for sentiment. It could just as easily have been us, that's war,' noted Clinch.

The crawl back was a long one. 'How intense is the pain, Frank?' asked Barton.

'So bad that I feel like asking you to shoot me. Only consolation is it will probably get me a holiday.'

As time went by and there was no rat-tat-tat from the machine gun, the Germans seemed to grow suspicious. Flares and shells went up more frequently and the retreating men had to continually bury their faces in the Flanders' mud. Fortunately, they were near their own line when they were finally spotted. Bullets zipped all around them, but their own men, now alerted to their return, gave them frantic covering fire. Clinch and Barton crawled with more urgency. Gill, showing a lack of experience, got up to limp the last few yards.

'For God's sake, Gill, get down!' yelled Leveridge. Too late.

No holiday, Gillie; not to be, thought Barton as he and Clinch gratefully sipped a ration of rum, sitting exhausted behind the wall of their trench.

***

As a leaden morning came with a promise of yet more rain, the soldiers set about getting breakfast. There was an understanding between both sides that in the morning there would be an unofficial truce for an hour to give the combatants a chance to have their meal. So, at a given sign, men would emerge like rats from the ground to gather firewood and forage for food. Often the meal might just consist of stale bread or a biscuit softened in water and washed down with a mug of tea, with some tea saved to be used later for washing or shaving purposes.

As the boys of 'B' Company were having breakfast (tea with bread, supplemented with some bully as a reward for the undoing of the lethal machine gun), a strange soldier entered the trench and joined the group. The remaining members of the section were all now present – Lance Corporal Percy Bentley from Essex, Private James McGovern born in Glasgow, Private Thomas Evans of Dublin and Private Edward McHugh, who always claimed that rebel leader Fiach McHugh O'Byrne, 'firebrand of the Wicklow mountains', was an ancestor. Those originating in England or Scotland usually had at least one parent from the Emerald Isle. Even Leveridge himself, despite being a product of Eton and Oxford, was the son of Mary Murphy from Ballydehob in County Cork, Ireland.

On first hearing that piece of news, Moore had cried out, 'Well fair play to you Mary Murphy for conquering them English strongholds.'

The whole group curiously eyed the stranger who had appeared in their midst. Leveridge hastened to explain. 'Men, this is Private Ned Stack, formerly of the Royal Munster Fusiliers. He has been transferred to the 2/Royal Dubliners to serve as a sniper. Owing to the busyness of the German snipers in our area, HQ felt we needed a hand and sent some sharp-shooters along from other battalions. He is from County Kerry. Back home he was a journalist on a local newspaper, so be careful about what you say!'

'From Kerry, sir, not Dublin. What a relief!' It was Furlong again.

'Relief!' cried Moore with mock indignation. 'Trouble with 'B' Company is that good Dublin stock is being completely watered down by inferior strains from elsewhere.'

'There's nothing inferior about this ingredient at any rate,' continued Leveridge. 'Private Stack is a survivor of the rearguard action from Etreux last August.'

'Etreux!' gasped the company, as though the word had mystical significance. The men knew that great deeds had been wrought there but, owing to all the pother of war that they themselves had endured, they were short on specifics.

'Tell us about it, Ned,' whispered Barton. 'Was it awful?'

'Horrendous but gallant,' began Stack, 'For bravery, it compares well with any action in the annals of war. When we arrived in Le Havre on August 13th, 2/Battalion Royal Munster Fusiliers was billeted at the village of Bone, three miles east of Etreux. After a stay of five days, we marched north to the Belgian frontier and remained in reserve while the fighting raged at Mons.

'During the next three days the retreat was carried out in fiercely hot weather. The reservists among us found it particularly tough what with having to lug heavy packs in addition to all the other hardships. But they stuck it out. Up to the 26th, the battalion had done no fighting and were restlessly waiting for an order to attack.

'Then on August 27th, all hell broke loose. We found ourselves having to halt the attack of an entire German army corps! In all probability, nothing like this had ever happened in modern warfare. Incredibly, lads, the 2/Munsters did it. During the rearguard action, lots of survivors fell back on an orchard by the main road near Etreux. Captain Hall of 'A' Company took command. Seeing the enemy pushing forward towards the east, he gave the order to engage. A small party then charged with determination. They were outnumbered fifty to one, but so great was their resolve that the Germans recoiled in the face of their fury. Having foiled repeated onslaughts, the little party retreated to the orchard.

'I was hidden in a disused machine-gun post above the orchard and could observe all that was happening. I had been doing my duty as a sniper there. At one point, an enemy soldier came towards the post to suss it out. Miraculously, he changed his mind. Its utterly wrecked state must have made the task seem unnecessary. I laid low in my isolated and exposed position throughout the action. To have done otherwise would have meant instant death. That night I would find my way back to our own lines under cover of darkness.

'The German army completely surrounded what remained of the battalion, whose machine guns had fallen silent. Ammunition spent. Lieutenant Chute, who was in charge of the machine guns, was shot and his place taken by Sergeant Johnson. He had his men continue firing their rifles until their last cartridge was gone. As bullets were running out, he had the guns systematically destroyed and did the same with the silenced machine guns. Left without hardly any ammunition, the survivors, sparing what they had, lined the four sides of the orchard. Against all the odds, they still kept the enemy at bay. As darkness fell, Johnson and his men realised that the situation was hopeless. At 9.15 p.m., four non-commissioned officers and 240 men surrendered. That was all that remained of the now immortal 2/Munsters Battalion. As the men surrendered, an awe-struck German army arrived on the scene.

'They were moved at the sight of the battered and bloodied remnant with dead and wounded strewn about the place. The heroes stood to attention as they submitted. Even the wounded who could do so struggled, or were helped, to their feet and held their heads high. The surrounding foe broke into applause. Their commanding officer shouted, 'Attention!' and they saluted the valour of these men. Johnson and his troops returned the gesture. But the German Corps commander must have been riled to discover that they had been utterly foiled by a mere battalion.

'Next morning the Germans found themselves fourteen hours behind in their offensive programme. Fourteen hours that could never be recovered. As for the Munsters, all that remained to be done was assist the wounded and bury the dead in a story now destined for the ages.'

A reverential silence followed Stack's account. What a story-teller, thought Barton. Then Leveridge remarked, 'You know how in the course of a sporting fixture there is an event that doesn't seem all that significant at the time, yet in the end is seen as the turning point of the game? Well, maybe the precious fourteen hours lost by the Germans at Etreux will in retrospect be seen as a significant turning point in this Great War game.' Stack, who had been a keen Gaelic footballer back in Kerry, could appreciate what the Lieutenant was saying.

'Men, breakfast "truce" will soon be at an end. Start to think of returning to your battle stations,' announced Clinch.

'Talking of truces, did you hear that the Pope has called for a Christmas truce?' asked Belford.

'Fat chance, George. The brass would never wear it,' said Clinch.

'A pity,' continued Belford. 'We've become quite pally with the boys opposite, what with our throwing bully, jam, biscuits and newspapers over to them and they throwing things back; they shouting "Hello Englander, Englander" and we answering "Good old Gerry". I'm sure they include us Irish. They even cry, "How was Gertie Miller and the Gaiety?" They know London well. Many worked there as waiters, barbers, taxi drivers and so on. And look how in certain slack moments we have played target competitions with them.'

'Maybe so, Belford, but the board has just gone up to indicate the end of the breakfast break,' said Clinch. 'Everyone resume your position.'

As though to emphasise what the Sergeant had said, a shell soon whined through the morning calm and burst on the far side of their trench, sending shrapnel flying above their heads. The war was once again in progress.

STAVE TWO

Christmas Eve

On Christmas Eve 1914, Lenny Barton was surveying No Man's Land from a support trench. A young English trooper of 5/London called Bassingham was the last one to be shot on the day. But that was hours earlier. Since then there had been a lull in hostilities.

Barton marvelled at the total transformation of the Western Front. Gone were the weeping skies and the slimy sea of devastation. As night fell, a burnished moon sang out in the star-freckled heavens and the glory of the stars pulsed emerald, ruby and sapphire from the patient infinity of space. No Man's Land looked like a scene from a Christmas card. The landscape of treacly mud that had engulfed men and animals for months had disappeared. So, too, had the shell-pocked vista with its upended duckboards and blasted trees. Even the dead sheep and humans that lay strewn about were changed – all changed – seeming like Christmas trees. Once sinister pools had become icy jewels in the moonlight. Everything was held fast in the iron grip of winter and all the jaggedness smoothened and sanitised by a heavy coat of gleaming rime.

For the first time in months Barton felt at peace, even though his heart ached for Eileen Walsh. Love for her had driven him into the army, a ploy he hoped would make it possible for him to marry her one day. If he survived. The situation that prevented their union seemed unsolvable, but in this enchanted moment he could not but hope. Eileen was always quoting some mystic to him who said, 'All will be well and all manner of things will be well.' He trusted Eileen. She was not only a beautiful girl, but also a wise one.

From the German trenches, a sonorous tenor voice rang out on the frigid air, *Stille Nacht, Heilige Nacht*. The conversations coming from both sides of No Man's Land, which carried well on a frosty night, ceased. It seemed as though the world listened, spellbound. As the last notes of the hymn faded away, the 2/Dubliners broke into rapturous and prolonged applause. *Silent Night*, they then decided, deserved a response. They sang *The First Nowell* and the Tommies along the front joined them.

The Germans followed this with *O Tannenbaum*. The Dubliners and other men of the British Expeditionary Force gave a stirring rendering of *O Come All Ye Faithful*, while the Germans joined in with the Latin version *Adeste Fideles*. Fritz persisted with the hymns and the Britishers regaled 'the foe' with *Pack Up Your Troubles, Tipperary* and *The Bonnie Banks of Loch Lomond*. Finally there was a mighty performance of '*Land of My Fathers*', particularly by the Welshmen present – shades of Cardiff for a Triple Crown showdown.

When the singing ceased, there were cries of 'Happy Christmas you Englishmen!', to which a Glaswegian of the Seaforths replied, 'Same to ye, Fritz, but dinna o'er eat yoursel' wi' the sausages!'

A solitary, lit-up Christmas tree appeared above the parapet of the foremost German trench, then another and yet another until they stretched along the front for a considerable distance. The clamped colourful candles seemed like footlights in a vast theatre. The Dubliners and their fellows gazed in awe at what would surely be (for those lucky enough to survive this war) a scene forever locked in the memory. All now clapped and cheered, not least Barton.

Now Barton and his pals were in for an even greater surprise. A German soldier – the one who had so gloriously sung *Stille Nacht* – got out of his trench, Christmas tree in hand, and stood there, tall. Everyone present held their breath. Only that day a warning of a surprise Christmas attack had been issued by Allied HQ in St Omer. Major General Wilson stressed the need to be alert. Despite this, no command was bellowed, no shot fired.

The soldier steadily marched out into No Man's Land and towards the British positions. He was soon joined by his companions. The 2/Dubliners and other Allies, too, poured out of their redoubts and went to meet the Germans midway between the lines. Baffled by what was happening, one soldier curiously stayed put – it was Thomas Evans of 'B' Company, 2/Royal Dublin Fusiliers. He was dubious about this outreach to the enemy.

Edward McHugh, descendant of the fearsome Fiach, was soon engaging with a German, who was showing him a photograph of three young women.

'I must say I fancy your eldest daughter,' blurted out the Dubliner.

'That's my wife,' said the German curtly.

'My God,' replied McHugh in dismay. 'I hope I'm not going to re-ignite the war.'

'Don't worry,' said Fritz and laughed heartily. 'She's going to be thrilled by your gaffe. The other two are my daughters. Now that's a different matter. They may go after you with rolling pins if they ever get the chance.'

'I wish I could speak German like you speak English. How come you're so fluent?'

'I was head waiter in the Great Central Hotel in London for years.'

Major John A. Burridge, also from 2/Royal Dublin Fusiliers, but from 'A' Company, found a German soldier looking at him intently. The major was somewhat embarrassed, because he had an angry scar from a wound that hadn't quite healed on his right cheek. The soldier approached him. He seemed apprehensive.

'My name is Hans Hoffman,' he announced.

'Pleased to meet you, Hans. Merry Christmas!'

'Same to you, sir.' He paused and pointed at the scar on the major's face and then astounded him by gingerly adding, 'I did that.'

'How on earth can you tell?'

'I'm a sniper. I remember your face vividly in the sights of my gun. Sorry, sir. Nothing personal.'

'I understand. But this is an amazing coincidence, Hans. Who would have thought we'd ever get a chance to know each other? Come, let us get our hands on a drink and talk some more ...'

For a short time, the horrors of war were left behind. Many of the Germans had a good grip on English and could speak for themselves or interpret for others. Some of them, like McHugh's contact, had worked in England. The celebrations were soon fuelled by schnapps, beer and even some fine Rhenish wines and, as they toasted each other, the chatter grew more animated, if sometimes less coherent. Cigarettes, tobacco and good German cigars were exchanged. The men also began to swap souvenirs: buttons, badges, caps, even the odd, deeply appreciated, spiked German helmet or picklehaube. There was music, too, as a mouth organ, bagpipes and violin appeared on the scene.

In the midst of all these celebrations and good fellowship a German captain raised his hands and eyes to heaven and pleaded, 'My God, why cannot we have peace and let us all go home?' Clearly all the men were already weary of the futile slaughter.

'Simple, sir,' volunteered Moore who was close by, 'The big wigs who started all this are thinking only about their power, lands and connollys overseas. They're not bothered about us poor sods.'

Barton, who overheard this, was wondering how the German was processing the 'connollys overseas', one of Moore's more amusing malapropisms, when he found himself standing before another officer.

'Nice meeting you,' said the stately man, extending a hand to Barton. 'Sewald, 48 Saxons.'

'Lenny Barton, 2/Royal Dublin Fusiliers, sir. Nice meeting you too.'

'The name is Rolf.'

Barton observed a fine, strong-boned face, and eyes that seemed to sparkle in the vivid moonlight. When a celebratory flare lit up No Man's Land, Lenny saw those eyes were dark and deep.

'So you're from Ireland?

'Yes, from County Kilkenny. A little town called Ballybeg.'

'Have you a family?'

'A brother and sister.'

'No wife? Don't tell me that a raven-haired, blue-eyed, hand-some fellow like you hasn't been hooked by some likely girl.'

'I'm a slippery fish.'

'So what's the story?'

Barton was warming to this man. It was something instinctive. Would he tell him? Oh, why not! 'I have been utterly frustrated in love,' he declared.

'How come?'

'You see, I'm a Protestant.'

'Didn't know that was a bar to romance.'

'If the one you love is an Irish Catholic, it is. You see I'm besotted with a neighbouring girl called Eileen Walsh and long to marry her, but this is a big no, no for her Catholic family. It's not accepted in Irish society, least of all in rural areas. Believe me, this situation has been the lot of many couples. It seems I'll have to turn if I want her as my wife. It's the only way.'

'Turn?'

'Convert to Catholicism.'

'Would that be the end of the world?'

'I'm Church of Ireland – Anglican – and that is my faith. I could not just become a Catholic to marry Eileen. It would not be sincere.'

'Why are the Catholics so obdurate?'

'History. They were downtrodden for centuries by their English Protestant masters. In actual fact, these were English settlers, as were my own family, the Bartons. Not all of them were bad. There were those among them who treated Catholics well and I'm pleased to say the Bartons would have been such. Those who have stayed generally have good relations with the locals nowadays. After all, it's centuries since the blow-ins blew in.'

'So what's the problem now?'

'History as I said. They say the English never remember their history and the Irish never forget it. There's some truth in that. Take my own town of Ballybeg in Kilkenny. What the English Lord Protector Oliver Cromwell did there is still vivid in the folk memory. In 1650 he besieged the town, which was very stoutly defended against his powerful army of Roundheads. About three hundred of his experienced soldiers were killed there, which did not amuse him. Locals still relate how he placed a cannon on the Moat and destroyed the nearby Augustinian Abbey. Indeed he left the whole town in ruins, killed many of the natives, banished still more and gave their lands to English Protestant settlers. Some of these Cromwellian settlers' names are still to be found there such as Lambert and Holden. A number of them have now become Catholics and more Irish than the Irish themselves. This ruthless pattern was repeated throughout Ireland.'

'But that happened in the seventeenth century,' Rolf observed.

'Well, as I said, the Irish have long memories. Then there was the appalling Famine in the 1840s, which was another episode that left an indelible mark on the Irish psyche. Tales are told of people being found dead, their mouths stained green by the grass they had been eating to assuage their ravaging hunger. And this happened in a situation where they would have been well fed with soup if they converted to Protestantism.'

'Is this take on history somewhat one-sided?'

'You have a point. The Protestants too have their bitter memories of brutal killings in Ulster during the Catholic Rebellion of 1641.'

'I can see how these key historic events can complicate personal lives, including your own, Lenny.'

'The long and the short of it is that if a Catholic has a mind to marry a Protestant or vice versa, these events surface from the dark depths of the folk memory and such a union can become a bridge too far for both parties, unless one is ready to surrender their beliefs and identity.'

'You say that Eileen's family are opposed to a marriage. What about your own?'

'They, too, are firmly against it, yet I feel that, in the end, I might be able to get around them.'

''Tis indeed a dilemma,' said Rolf Sewald.

'It's the reason why I joined the British army and find myself bogged down in Flanders.'

'What do you mean?'

'Jack Walsh, Eileen's father, is an ardent supporter of Home Rule for our country and one of the reasons why Irishmen are taking part in this war is to win Home Rule. It will bring about a great measure of autonomy for Ireland. And I'm hoping that my sacrifice will soften his stance on the marriage issue. You know, although he wouldn't have me as a son-in-law, he and I are quite friendly.'

'I hope your plan works out, Lenny. And perhaps this Armageddon is going to affect things. It may lead to a world where attitudes will change completely.'

'I think you may be right.'

'I sincerely hope so for your sake.'

'And you know something else? And this is rather odd. You, a German, are the first one I have told my story of forlorn love to on this front.'

'Thanks for having confidence in me. Remember it was the Samaritan who came to the aid of the poor Jewish fellow who was beaten up and robbed on the road to Jericho. Not the holy fellows.'

'Thanks for listening, Rolf.'

Taking a photograph from his wallet, Rolf said, 'Hey Lenny, you must meet the family.'

'You men love to show off photographs of your families.'

'It's where the heart is, after all, especially at Christmas.'

In the photograph with Rolf was his comely wife and two fair-haired teenage sons.

'Good photo, Rolf. Nice family.'

'My wife is called Aga, and the boys are Friedrich and Walter. Walter is the younger one. Friedrich is studious and fond of music – he plays the violin well. Walter is the sportsman. He'd play football all day long, if Aga wasn't there to make him think of even more important things. She keeps the boys at it in my absence.'

Seeing that the boys were getting up in their teens, Lenny asked, 'Don't you worry about them eventually getting trapped in this war?'

'It does worry me. But I think it will end quickly. We have the high ground and are well dug in. I think the Allies will tire of hurling themselves at our defences and make peace. That's our best hope. If that doesn't happen, then I don't know where all this will go. Even if we were to drive the British into the sea, they would still control that sea and the torment would go on. We couldn't sustain that.'

'But those in power have an appetite for war. They have vested interests in all of this.'

'Yet what interests most of us meeting here on this blessed night? Home and family, of course, and the desire for this to end, so that we can go home and get on with our ordinary lives. I'm beginning to have grave doubts about this whole conflict.'

In the silence that followed, Lenny heard a purring sound and felt a cat brushing against the leg of his trousers. He looked down at the grey cat, its fetching coat traversed by dark tigerish stripes. 'Hello, Korky. How did you get here?'

'You know this cat?' asked Rolf.

'Yes, he visits our trench from time to time, mewing for food. Has a great fondness for bully, never tires of it. I can tell you he's unique in that respect.'

'Oh, we know him too. He's a frequent visitor. We don't call him K—? What's that you called him?'

'Korky.'

'We call him Lazarus – Laz for short. He can demolish a tasty piece of sausage in double-quick time also.'

'Lazarus? That's an odd sort of name for a cat.'

'In one of your bombardments we saw him take what looked like a direct hit, but when the dust settled, out he crawled from underneath a mound of clay. So we called him Lazarus, didn't we Laz? Like the man who came back from the dead in the Good Book.'

Yes you did and the name was more appropriate than you knew, Rolf. When I was a kitten, the farmer in whose barn I was born took me and my siblings to a nearby stream to drown us, because, as he told his weeping son, 'The farmyard was overrun with bloody cats.' Me and my brothers and sisters didn't know at the time where we were going and were all jostling about in the sack. Imagine the shock when we hit the icy water! In desperation we scrambled, scratched and strove to escape as we suffocated. The bag somehow opened as a result of our despairing efforts. I swam towards the water's edge and clambered onto the bank. 'My God,' cried the farmer, 'that little blackguard has escaped!' And he scurried along the bank. No doubt he wanted to grab me and return me to a watery grave. With a toe, the boy surreptitiously edged a huge sod into the path of his father, who toppled over and fell centimetres short as he was about to grasp my tail. I staggered, cold and sodden, into the shelter of some nearby bushes. 'Give him a chance, Dad,' pleaded the boy, 'He's a plucky little fellow.' The man looked wryly at his son. 'He's lucky that sod was in

*the way, Pierre.' Yet he gave me my chance. So you may well call
me Lazarus, Rolf.*

Barton gently picked up the cat and looked into his face. 'You
know, Rolf, I think you're right. Lazarus is a perfect name for him.
Only the other day I saw – '

Before Lenny could finish his story, loud cheers and whistles
broke out behind him. Turning towards the noise, he spotted Sean
Furlong with his arms in the air.

'Sean, what's happening?'

'The officers have agreed to extend the truce.'

Barton roared with delight. 'I can hardly believe it. How long?
How long will the truce last?'

'At least until St Stephen's Day. Then they'll review the situ -
ation.'

'But will HQ agree? What if they send orders to attack?'

'If they do, we'll first direct warning shots into the air.'

'I pray such orders will not be given.'

'Me too,' agreed Rolf. 'Peace for Christmas is wonderful news.
It's the best gift I've ever received. Merry Christmas, Lenny!'

'Merry Christmas to you too, Rolf. And many of them. See you
tomorrow.'

Barton picked up the cat. 'Come on, Lazarus, you are also invited
to whatever is happening tomorrow. You better come back to the
trenches and get some sleep first.'

*I like this man. He often says he's a Kilkenny cat, whatever that is –
must be some sort of nickname – but he doesn't seem to know much
about cats. We don't waste time sleeping at night. We hunt. And
with all the rodents around here, a cat is kept busy. Mind you,
hunting is not what it used to be. The rats are huge and savage and
well able to hunt us! Imagine. What's the world coming to?*

***

Far back in the German reserve trenches, a trooper was at a small
table working on a painting.

Another soldier who had just entered took a look. 'Not bad at
all,' he commented. 'What is that building?'

'Thank you, Private Schmidt. It's not often genius is recognised.'

Schmidt laughed. He hadn't quite said that, but he knew the artist wasn't lacking in self-confidence.

'It's Messines Church. I worked on it when I was in the crypt, recovering from wounds.'

'Great steeple.'

'Yes, it is quite soaring and majestic. An outstanding landmark. It's taken something of a battering since,' observed the artist, who was a smallish man with a full black moustache, an unkempt thatch of hair, beady eyes and a somewhat comical nose.

'Did you hear the news about the camaraderie between our soldiers and the enemy in No Man's Land?'

'Unhappily, I did.'

'Unhappily?'

'Yes. This celebration over what is nothing but a Christian myth in the first place is preposterous. All that story about a virgin birth, a manger, shepherds, wise men and angels is nonsense. It's a Jewish conspiracy to weaken our resolve so that we lose the war,' said the artist.

'You are totally obsessed with the Jews, Adolf. If we were to have a blizzard tonight, I swear you'd blame it on the Jews. It's not rational.'

'Don't be a fool, Schmidt. They are an inferior race that will corrupt our German Empire and the world, if we don't take radical action to stop the filthy apes!' he shouted hypnotically, eyes flashing. 'Those antics in No Man's Land are just humbug. Worse still they are treasonous.'

Schmidt had heard that Adolf Hitler's grandfather was a Jew and had been about to innocently query him on the matter. Owing to the extreme vehemence of this outburst, he thought better of it. Instead he said rather incongruously that he would go and get some fresh air, though he had just arrived to enjoy the warmth of the stonehouse. No doubt about it – Adolf was a strange fellow.

***

Elsewhere, Tommies hastily summoned their mates from the support and reserve trenches farther back to 'come and see this thing that has come to pass'. There had not been such amazing happenings since the notable goings on in Bethlehem nearly two thousand years before. Surveying those sights in the sweet moonlight, they raised their eyes to the skies, expecting to hear choirs of angels sing:

Glory to God in the highest
And peace on earth to men of goodwill.

And some of them did.

STAVE THREE

Christmas Morning

Lenny Barton surveyed the scene on Christmas morning. The fog that enveloped the Western Front, exaggerating the proportions of the men who, Magwitch-like, lumbered about, looked as though it would make way for another crystalline day.

The customary arrangement of allowing a space for breakfast was reinforced by the truce. The meal had also been enhanced for this special occasion and the air was filled with the delicious smell of frying bacon and sizzling eggs. This was sheer luxury to the war-battered troops.

Following the hearty breakfast, Barton noted a definite change of atmosphere. Germans and British alike – suspending the mood of celebration – turned to a solemn duty. Strewn on that Flanders field were a hundred or more of their dead comrades awaiting decent burial. The digging of the graves in the unyielding ground proved arduous, and committing their comrades to the earth harrowing, but no one shirked the task.

On one side of the burial site were the British, on the other the Germans: all heads were uncovered, all stood erect and reverent. The officers of both sides were to the front. Father Ryan, positioned between the serried ranks, eloquently enunciated the Twenty-third Psalm. He delivered it in English, and a German named Heinrich Appel, who was training for ministry, spoke it in his own native tongue:

> The Lord is my shepherd: I shall not want.
> He maketh me to lie down in green pastures:
> He leadeth me beside the still waters.

> *De Herr is mein Hirt: mir wird nichts mangeln.*
> *Er weidet mich auf einer grünen Aue:*
> *Und führt mich zum frischen Wasser.*

The chaplain then saluted the German troops and withdrew. Appel did the same with the British. The parties dispersed in silence.

Barton had watched in awe as these supposedly sworn enemies stood reverently together in prayer. He and Eileen frequently
exchanged letters. Soon after the event, one of them said, 'If I
hadn't seen this for myself, I could never have believed it.'

'I'm frozen after all that standing and I could eat a horse,' said
Clinch, as they returned from the solemnities.

Stack rubbed his hands in anticipation, 'Time to dig into all
those goodies that came in the Christmas and Princess Mary
parcels – Horlicks, Bovril, turkey, hams, plum puddings, plum-
duff...'

'Stop it! This is torture,' complained Furlong.

'And Sergeant,' continued Stack, 'you will be able to wrap up
in the scarves, caps, pullovers, mittens and so forth. That'll keep
you snug.'

'I'm dying for a cigarette or a tot of rum or whisky at the
minute,' declared Furlong, 'Aren't you, Evans?' This he said to
tease Private Thomas Evans, who was a surly and withdrawn sort
of fellow and a joyless Christian. For him it was the letter of the
law, not the spirit. Although he did not join in the celebration on
Christmas Eve, he had no qualms about the religious service.

'I don't smoke and I don't drink. And I think everybody would
be better off without these evils,' snapped Evans.

'Ah, Tom, I think you may have a point on cigarettes, but a little
drop of liquor is okay for most people. Everything in moderation.
After all, St Paul says, "A little wine is good for the stomach" and
the Man himself provided the wine for the first cocktail party,' answered Furlong.

'The devil can quote scripture for his own purposes,' retorted
Evans, as they entered the trench.

'Trouble with you, Evo, is that there is no give in you.
Everything is black and white. No shades of grey.'

'If it was me, Furlong, I'd resemble that comparison with the
devil.' It was Moore giving a fair approximation once again!

'Talking of smokes,' said Clinch, 'those cigars the Germans
gave us this morning weren't half bad. And the cognac was sup -
erb. Just for some variety at Yuletide, I'd sure like to get my hands
on their parcels of goose, venison, fondue, carp, cinnamon biscuits, candy apple –'

'And good red wine, Tom Evans,' added Furlong.

'Umph!' exclaimed a grumpy Evans.

'But they won't be getting a Christmas card from King George and Queen Mary. Nor greetings from the Princess. My mother will be as proud as punch,' said Bentley, who wished he was home with his mum in Essex.

Their anticipation of Christmas dinner only ended when Leveridge arrived.

'Thought you'd been taken prisoner, Lieutenant,' said Stack.

'No such luck. But I do have a wonderful surprise for you all.'

He stepped aside to allow Michael Cochrane to enter the trench. He had recovered somewhat from his ordeal with the rat – regretfully there was no furlough. Leveridge summed up the feelings of all, saying: 'Michael you are as welcome as the flowers in May! It's lovely to have you back, and on such an auspicious occasion.'

'Yes, and you're just in time for dinner!' said Barton, as he hugged his is fellow townsman.

STAVE FOUR

Christmas Dinner

Leveridge and his men intended to conduct dinner in style. And even had a menu made out, which was generally authentic, though a little garnished in places. It read:

HORS D'OEUVRES
Sardines

SOUP
Turtle – Ivelcon – Oxo

FISH
Herrings

ENTREE
Meat and Vegetable Ration (consisting of Tinned Beef,
Potatoes, Carrots, Beans, Onions and Gravy)

POULTRY
Turkey (Devilled or Roast)

SWEETS
Christmas Pudding (hot and alight with rum) and Mince Pies

SAVOURY
Bread and Butter and Bloater Paste and Pâté de Fois Gras

DESSERT
Dates, Figs, Apples, Almonds and Raisins, Preserved Ginger,
Mixed Chocolates,
Black Coffee – Cocoa – Café au lait Marrons Glacés

LIQUERS
Cognac Rum
Crackers and Cigars

The toasts were:

Ireland
Dublin
The King
The Other Sections
The People at Home
The wounded in Hospital
and
A Silent Toast for those who have gone under.

'Let's get started,' said Moore. 'I can't wait for that "Gras" stuff.'

'Go on out of that, Moore. 'Twas far from *pâté de fois gras* you were reared,' Clinch was ribbing his old mate.

'The cheek of you,' retorted Moore. 'Didn't me ancestors survive on plates of fried grass, or whatever you call it, during the Famine?'

'Now, now, men,' intervened McGovern with mock solemnity, 'Think of the day that's in it. Peace on earth to men of goodwill and all that.'

'Sure Clinchie would try the patience of a saint never mind a fellow of goodwill.'

'You should take a leaf out of Laz's book here,' said Barton, who had the cat nestling beside him.

'His name is Korky,' corrected Belford, who in general was content to listen.

'No, George. I've discovered that his original name was Laz. So Laz he is. But look what I found secreted in his collar.' He produced a note that read, 'Nollaig shona dhíbh, Irishmen, from the Saxons.'

'What does that mean?' enquired Bentley. 'My German is rusty.'

'It's not your German that's rusty, Corporal. It's your Irish. It means Happy Christmas,' replied an amused Barton. 'Did your Irish mammy not tell you?'

'Well done, old Gerries,' exclaimed Bentley.

'I think Laz is an example to us in the way he has crossed No

Man's Land and reached out to the enemy,' said Stack, 'A pity men can't learn from creatures.'

'Some tribute,' muttered Evans caustically, 'I wonder what else is hidden in his collar as he comes and goes.'

'That sounds ominous,' noted Stack, calmly enough.

The other diners, however, bristling with hostility, glared at Evans.

Barton, normally a placid man, was aroused. 'Evans, what sort of a twisted mind do you have that gives a nasty slant to such a noble gesture?' This was said without much venom, but Evans behaviour was astounding.

He jumped to his feet and unsheathed a knife. 'Twisted mind! How dare you! I'll show you –'

'Private Evans! Drop that knife. It's an order,' yelled Lieutenant Leveridge, 'Remember the day that's in it.'

Evans obeyed slowly and sullenly, casting resentful glances at Barton.

The violent reaction shocked Barton. 'Peace, Evans. Let it be,' he said quietly.

There was a grudging 'okay' from Evans, but he still smouldered over his soup.

Must have recalled a bitter memory that touched some deeply sensitive nerve or some such, thought Barton.

'Ah come on men,' urged Moore, 'the Lieutenant is right. This is no day to upset the rhubarb tart. Let's make the most of it and enjoy ourselves. Who knows what tomorrow will bring?'

That brought a rumble of agreement from the men.

As the meal progressed, Barton was struck by the relish with which these soldiers worked their way through the menu after months of cruel deprivation and a surfeit of bully, Maconochie's stew (often cold when they managed to get it) and Tickler's so-called jams. The cognac, rum, crackers and cigars at the end really crowned a scrumptious meal.

'I wish we had a drop of the black stuff,' lamented Moore, as they were enjoying their drinks, 'That would really bring us back home.'

'Talking of Guinness, did you ever hear the story of the worker who fell into a great vat of porter at St James's Gate in Dublin?' asked Furlong.

'No, what happened?' asked Bentley.

'Well,' Furlong continued, 'realising he couldn't swim, his pals rushed to the side of the gigantic vat to pull him out. But he wasn't surfacing. And the level of the porter was going down. At last he broke the surface of the heavenly elixir, raised his eyes to the sky and cried, "O God, give me a mouth worthy of this occasion." And with that he dived underneath once more – with enthusiasm.'

'That's hilarious,' roared Bentley, slapping his knee. 'If ever I'm elected to Westminster, I'll open my maiden speech to parliament with that story.'

Following the jollity and warmth of the meal, some of the toasts were edged with sadness. When 'The People at Home' were remembered, thoughts raced to children, wives, sweethearts, fathers, mothers, siblings and friends in faraway places. People they might never see again.

Barton's heart went out to his beloved Eileen. He dwelt on their walks by the waters of the Avonree in Ballybeg, through the Abbey Meadow and down along Butler's Grove and the Furry Knock with their carpet of buttercups, daisies, bluebells and primroses. Above all, he recalled the time spent under the great oak tree, entwined in each other's arms, often uttering sweet nothings, which didn't matter anyway. It was all about intimacy. He sighed deeply at the thought.

Then came a toast to 'The Boys in the Firing Trenches' in the knowledge that in some parts of the front, where there was no truce, men would die even on this sacred day.

'A Silent Toast for those who have gone under' proved the most poignant moment of all. Captains Byrne and McGuinness fondly came to mind, as did the hapless Frank Gill and, oh, so many others.

Following a minute of respectful and profound silence, Clinch, who had proposed the toast, finished with 'May they rest in peace.' To which all responded, 'Amen.'

For a while the atmosphere was subdued as their thoughts

went back to the casualties of war. Then Bentley quietly asked, 'Why did we let ourselves get involved in this catastrophe?'

'Hunger!' exclaimed Evans, 'In my case it was hunger. I was part of a big family living in the squalor of a Dublin tenement on Henrietta Street. It was a question of join up or starve.'

Maybe that explains a few things about you, thought Barton, and mitigates what one might think.

'What Thomas is saying is that he needed the work. The same would be true of Clinchie and myself,' added Moore.

'Hey Moore,' said Clinch, 'I haven't lost my tongue and can speak for myself.'

'If only you would lose your tongue, it would give us all a rest. What I'm trying to say is that we are career soldiers. We definitely joined for the work. You know something, before I enlisted I was unemployed for so long that I thought Manual Labour was the President of Spain.'

'He's right you know,' said Clinch – unexpectedly.

'I guess I joined for the lark,' said Furlong, 'Carlow didn't seem the centre of the universe and I was looking for adventure. Tell you something though, I'd give anything to be back in dear old Carlow now.'

'Cripes, you're easily pleased, Furlong. If it was Dublin, I'd understand. But Carlow!'

'Don't be smart, Clinch. Everyone knows that the best thing about Dublin is the road to Carlow,' retorted Furlong, 'Aren't you Dublin Jackeens always singing *Follow me down to Carlow*?'

'I joined up to win a bride.' It was Lenny Barton.

Leveridge smiled. This riddle regarding the 'bride' again, I must get to the bottom of this, he decided.

'Looking for a bride,' exclaimed Stack, 'Tell us more.'

'No. But there were other reasons also. I share the ideals proposed by John Redmond: the freedom of small nations, Home Rule for Ireland, support for the beleaguered Belgians ...'

'Apart from the bride bit. Those were pretty well my own reasons too,' nodded Stack.

'My friends went to war and I went with them,' admitted Belford.

'As for me,' Leveridge noted, 'I was naively patriotic. The

principals in this conflict drifted needlessly into war and I drifted with them.'

The men fell silent. Each reflecting on his own path to Flanders, while being impressed by the honesty of their Commanding Officer.

'Okay then. Let's meet Gerry in No Man's Land and see what shenanigans the afternoon holds,' said Leveridge.

'Good idea,' they chorused, and started moving in that direction. Evans hesitated, but then joined them, looking like a schoolboy creeping unwillingly to school. His going was tentative.

STAVE FIVE

Christmas Afternoon

When the men from 'B' Company got out into the centre of No Man's Land, the fraternisation between Tommy and Fritz was in full swing. Knowing that lean days were looming ahead, they generously exchanged the foodstuffs they had received for the festival. The British doled out bully beef, Maconochie's stew, biscuits, chocolate, Christmas pudding, rum, etc.; and the Germans: venison, sausages, sauerkraut, nuts, sweets, chocolates , etc. Inevitably they also shared photos of loved ones.

A German soldier looking at his gifts of food declared, 'These will make a pleasant change from the eternal turnips.'

As on the previous night, there were cigars and Rhenish wine aplenty. A Tommy remarked on the excellence of the wine.

To prove the point, a soldier from the Rhineland, who gave his name as Karl Niemann, recited a German saying: 'If you have been on the banks of the Rhine and you have not seen the Rhine, then you have been on the banks of the Rhine.'

'I don't understand,' said the Tommy.

'You'd be so sozzled with drinking the excellent wine, that you wouldn't even notice the mighty river,' explained Niemann patiently.

The German cigars got a mixed reaction. 'I think they're fam - ous,' was the verdict of Wicklow man, McHugh.

'There's no use arguing about taste,' said Glaswegian McGovern, 'because I would find them vile.'

Evans, who had come reluctantly out into No Man's Land, now became deeply disturbed. He began to feel that all this brotherly exchange of gifts would later be considered as collaboration with the enemy and severely reprehensible. He quietly sneaked back to his trench to sit out the rest of the day brooding, not doubting that Field Marshal French, Commander-in-Chief of the British Expeditionary Force, would see things his way.

Following Niemann's witty saying, the humour continued to flow. A group, mostly German, had gathered around storyteller

Furlong: 'There were some Kerry fellows – cute devils if ever I met them – who used to play a trick on you poor lads,' he began. 'Kerry, by the way, is a county in the southwest of Ireland, a very scenic place. You should go and enjoy it when this war ends. But, as I was saying, some Kerry blades used to play tricks on your lads. You see one of them would shout out "Hans!" from his trench – a common German name as you know – and a German would pop his head out of his dugout and shout back "Ja!" and be shot. Of course after a while your boys cottoned on to this and said, "These Irish'll find out that they have opened a Pandora's box for themselves", and so they made a plan. They found that the most common name among the Irish was Paddy, so didn't one of them cry out "Paddy!" and didn't the Kerry fellow keep his head down and yell back, "That you, Hans?" "Ja!" cried poor Hans, popping up his head.'

The Germans laughed heartily at this. They were good sports.

As the tempo of the occasion rose, fuelled by liquid nourishment, Moore declared it to be 'almighty craic'.

'And what is craic?' enquired Karl Niemann.

'A Gaelic word that means great fun entirely. In Ireland we love getting together to share stories, play music, sing songs and so forth,' explained Moore.

Then, as on the previous night, they joined together in *O Come All Ye Faithful*, the British in English, the Germans in Latin. The Irish for the most part joined Fritz by singing in Latin, as they had always done at Midnight Mass back in Ireland. Most of them didn't know the English version.

An amazing German juggler then performed. In the end he had so many coloured balls in the air that the onlookers were mesmerised and burst into loud and spontaneous applause.

Next up was a group of musicians with a few mouth organs giving a rendering of Beethoven's majestic *Hymn to Joy*.

'Sounded a bit thin on the mouth organs,' commented Captain Rolf Sewald.

'Great craic,' shouted Niemann, showing that he was a fast learner.

A Saxon comedian then appeared dressed in a skirt, blouse, bow tie, cone-shaped hat and carrying a motley, broken umbrella.

Even his appearance provoked laughter. He went about hatless for a while and pretended that a passing bird had done its business on his head. Whereupon he put an alarmed hand to the supposed mush and cried out in great distress, 'Someone's blown my brains out!'

British troops weighed in with the *Boys of Bonnie Scotland, O, O Antonio, It's a long way to Tipperary* and *Good King Wenceslas*. While, on request, the Germans sang *Stille Nacht* as on the Eve.

A highlight was a man who appeared carrying a wooden platform, which he placed on the ground. He doubled his left leg at the knee and strapped it up, so that he was perched on one leg. 'I am the one-legged champion tap dancer of all Bavaria,' he announced to laughter. The troops nearly fell over with mirth at his performance, which is what actually happened to the fellow himself!

A group struck up *Flower of Scotland* on the bagpipes, which not surprisingly frightened a hare from among some cabbages that had survived bombardments. A scattering of Seaforth Highlanders set off in wild pursuit. They very nearly upended a German (by trade a barber) who was giving a haircut to one of the Tommies.

'Jock, di' ye' nae feel the draught?' yelled Furlong. But their minds were too intent on a pot of savoury hare soup to engage in banter over wearing kilts.

While all this communal glee was in full flow and people were becoming better acquainted, little clusters formed here and there as the men began to chat more intimately.

Some conversations were limited because of language problems. Not so the parley between Leveridge and the Fritz who amazed him with the greeting, 'Watcha cock, how's London?'

This was not the Oxford man's natural idiom, but he responded gamely, 'I expect it's still there. But you astound me. You, a German, speaking in the Cockney dialect.'

'That's because I am a Cockney.'

'Then what are you doing in that uniform? Are you in disguise?'

'I'm a Saxon Londoner.'

'Not Anglo Saxon, I take it.'

He laughed. 'No, I'm from Saxony in Germany. I was born there, but my parents brought me to London soon after birth. They had a business in the East End – Bermondsey. I was reared in England and went to school there, but I wasn't ever naturalised, so I had to go back to Germany to do three years military service. Once finished, I returned to London and got a job on the railways. When the war came, I was called up by the German army – hence the disguise. My girlfriend, Daisy, is still in Bermondsey.'

'Your take on Cockney is as good as that of a pearly king, Fritz.'

'Cor blimey, mate, what did you expect? The name is Harry (Heinz in German) Bachmann.'

'Mine's Patrick, Patrick Leveridge from Hampshire.'

'Patrick? Paddy?'

'Irish mother.'

'You didn't get your accent from her.'

'No, she speaks with a musical Cork lilt, boy.'

'Oh, so that's it. That's an interesting uniform. You're an officer.'

'Yes, for my sins.'

'It's not easy, is it?'

'No, Harry, but many of my companions from Oxford ended up in the same plight. So many veteran officers were killed that people like us, without any great experience, were drafted. Mind you, we all joined this show with enthusiasm, not wanting to miss the fun.'

'The fun!'

'I'm revising my opinion. More and more it all seems sense-less. Many of my fellow students are dead. But I feel a commit-ment to my men. Most of them are great people. I have a desire to see them safely through this catastrophe. The real issues involved are not too relevant to them.'

Harry looked at the young face of this tall, dark-haired man and felt a surge of pity for him. He was so young and had to shoul-der such heavy responsibilities. Yet, because of his class, he could not be too familiar with the ordinary trooper. It had to be quite a lonely existence. He felt he must brighten up the situation for him.

They went on to talk of the Cup Final at Wembley (even sang a few bars of *Abide with Me*); the Ashes at the Oval; Gertie Miller at the Gaiety of course; barrowloads of purplish red plums, full of clammy nectar, on a sunny Borough High Street in August; summer outings to the sea at Brighton; and Dickensian, snow-adorned, carol-filled Christmases ...

They both enjoyed the reminiscing. The memories transported them back to dearly loved people and places on this translucent festival day and all but overwhelmed them with nostalgia.

Before parting, Bachmann gave Leveridge a bottle of Glenfiddich Scotch. 'Our lads are into schnapps, not whisky. It's a really good malt whisky actually.'

'I know it.'

'And you can keep that shapely bottle as a souvenir of this day.'

'That I will and thank you, Harry.'

A decent sort, thought Harry, as he walked away.

***

Not far away, Barton and Sewald had sought each other out.

'Happy Christmas again, Lenny.'

'Same to you, Rolf. Hope you're enjoying the celebrations.'

'So, so.'

'Oh?'

'Got a bit of bad news in a letter from Aga.'

'So sorry to hear that.'

'Walter, my sporting son, had a nearly fatal attack of diphtheria, which left him extremely weak. However, he's now recovering.'

'Oh, thank God.'

'It set me thinking about what we said yesterday regarding the futility of war. It's life on hold. The real concerns are home, family, community – Life is all about relationships.'

'Amen, to that,' said Barton, as he thought longingly of Eileen.

'Changing the subject,' said Sewald, 'I talked to a fellow officer last night who is a great student of English history. You know he had quite a different slant on Cromwell from you. Said he is regarded as the Father of English Democracy.'

'Yes, that is the English historical perspective, but not one we

Irish share, since he set out to obliterate us. I don't think any race would have a crush on someone who set out to do that.'

'But you are a Protestant.'

'I'm Anglican, Rolf. Cromwell wasn't mad about Anglicans either.'

'His tastes didn't seem to extend to a wide spectrum.'

'No, he was narrowly fundamentalist. Such people can be a menace. Irrational. By the way, there's a man in our section, Evans, who worries me a bit. Seems to deeply resent me for a remark not spoken with dire intent. He too would be a fundamentalist.'

'So Cromwell is not very popular in Ireland,' concluded Sewald.

'Certainly not. In fact there is an anecdote about an Irish parliamentarian called Tim Healy that bears this out. It seems that some Lord passed away in England, who was no friend of Ireland. Tributes were being paid to him in the House of Commons, when Healy growled audibly, "He's gone where Cromwell has gone!" Whereupon there were outraged cries of "Withdraw! Withdraw!" Healy waited for the uproar to die down and then, following a dramatic pause, remarked, "Gentlemen, you all seem pretty sure where Cromwell has gone!" Poor old Oliver. That place wouldn't exactly be a tourist destination.'

Just then a pigeon skimmed their heads and landed at some distance.

'Have you noticed how the birds have come back, now that the uproar of war has stopped?' asked Sewald, 'Earlier, I heard a robin sing its heart out on the frost-coated stump of a tree. If painted, it would make a good Christmas card. A passing Tommy said jokingly, "Shut up you fool! Don't you know it's the middle of winter?" The robin ignored him and carried on with its glorious melody. Rightly so.'

'Actually, the robin is one bird who continues singing in winter. Some say that he is merely staking out his territory, but I wouldn't like to agree with that Freudian version.'

'It would be wonderful if the bird song were to go on and the killing stop forever. But we will inevitably go back to killing each other. That's why I'd like to give you this as a remembrance. He presented him with a handsome badge with the distinctive German cross on it.'

'Thank you. I'll treasure it always.'

The two men then sadly decided to part, having more people to greet. They embraced and went their separate ways.

STAVE SIX

Laz and Cher Ami

Laz, tail erect, walked happily among the celebrating soldiers of both sides, who fed him titbits and frequently stroked and cuddled him. He was enjoying one such cuddle when a feathery movement caught his attention. A pigeon had landed out in the open. Following all the contact with humans, he felt eager to approach a creature more like his own kind.

The pigeon regarded Laz with an apprehensive cocked eye. The cat seemed benign and didn't come in stalking mode, otherwise he would have flown away. As it was he stood warily at the ready. He had a clear memory of a cat leaping from a shrub and grabbing one of those cousins of his who forage for food around city squares.

'Merry Christmas, pigeon.'

That was reassuring. 'Same to you, but I'm a dove.'

High notions, he's as 'pigeony' a pigeon as I've ever seen, but to avoid an argument a dove he will be … 'Well then,' said Laz, 'your coming is entirely appropriate to this place and in these circumstances. My name is Lazarus, Laz for short.'

'What an odd name. Why does it remind me of death?'

'I have no idea,' Laz lied, 'May I ask your name?'

'Cher Ami. It's a beautiful name.'

He certainly doesn't undersell himself. 'Indeed it is a lovely name and I hope we can become friends.'

'Creatures of our two species don't usually become friends. You're a cat, and as you've already noted, I'm a dove.'

I did no such thing. Why doesn't he get real? Maybe he's a snob who wants to distance himself from those grubby relatives on city squares. He's an ordinary black and grayish pigeon and none too plump. Well kept, but scrawny for all that. 'You could do with putting on a few ounces.'

'You're getting personal, feline, and you're certainly no diplomat.'

I'm no diplomat. Strewth! 'No offence, but for a pige … dove you're quite thin.'

'It's all the flying.'

I'm glad to see him become a tad more forthcoming. 'What is it you do?'

'Since the outbreak of the war, homing pigeons from all over England are being trained as carrier pigeons for use at the front. We were brought over here to experience the field of operations. I'm so glad there's a truce, because in the war I tend to keep my head down and not take any risks. I suppose I'm a bit of a coward really.'

Laz noted the touch of humility and the implicit admission that he was, after all, a pigeon. The impression was marred somewhat when he went on to say, 'What I'd really like to be is an eagle or a swallow.'

'A curious combination.'

'Well, I have a tremendous admiration for swallows. Their sense of direction is uncanny and the distances they travel immense. Our limit as carriers is something just over one thousand miles, while those slight little fellows travel many thousands. Some flying from the southern-most tip of Africa, for example, have ended up in Siberia. Astounding! The eagle, of course, is the King of the Birds.'

'Oh no he's not! The wren is. Have you not heard that there was once a great competition to decide who was King of the Birds? And they agreed that whoever could fly the highest would be King? The eagle, as he thought, climbed highest of all and declared himself King. Then a little voice came from higher up crying, "You are not. I am." It was one of the smallest of all birds – the wren. What happened was that, as the eagle set off, the wren hitched a lift on his tail and, when the great bird had reached his maximum height, the wren took off and flew higher. And so, the triumphant wren was crowned King of the Birds.'

'That's a great story. By the way, you haven't told me what you do yourself,' said Cher Ami.

'I'm what the Americans, who may one day join us in this war, would call a "bum". I befriend humans, Allied and German, in the hope that it might induce them to do the same with one another.'

'That's good. Why then do you say you're a "bum"?'

'I scrounge food from them, which helps me to avoid the monster rats. They'd eat you without salt. I survive on this battlefield; I'm a born survivor, but I'll not go into that.'

A hint of empathy appeared in the dark eyes of Cher Ami. 'I, too, am a survivor. There were two chicks in the nest: a male – myself – and a female called Paloma. Well, I was the weakling of the brood and only kept alive by the tender care of my handler. He fed me the choicest of grain, gave me water with a syringe and kept me cosy in the loft. That's why I'm here with you today.'

'I'm so glad you came to visit,' said Laz.

'Aren't we a strange couple though?' chortled Cher Ami.

'You're right you know. We too have had to meet across a kind of No Man's Land,' the cat laughed.

'I have to be getting back to my loft. There's a billing and cooing contest later.'

Laz was sorry to see Cher Ami leave so soon. He had felt a strange liking for the fellow and had a longing to know more about him. The pigeon seemed a complex mixture of conceit, naivety, humility, snobbery, bravery, brashness, timidity, honesty … In short he was an immature youngster. And yet Laz intuited something special about him. He hoped he hadn't heard the last of him.

As for Cher Ami, he had every intention of returning.

STAVE SEVEN

Germany v. The Western Isles

Looking around, Laz found soldiers from both sides milling about, wildly pursuing and kicking a football. Barton, watching in amusement, was reminded of small children who, when playing 'footer', all flock after the ball, wherever it goes, without any sense of position. An imposing Sergeant Major of the 1/Hampshires called Field, who in civvy street was a policeman and no stranger to point duty, must have had a similar thought. He offered to direct the traffic.

With everyone laughing, gasping and perspiring, Field's stentorian voice demanded, 'Stop, stop. Let you all stop!' Which they did. 'We must organise a proper international.'

'But Sergeant Major, who'll play in the game?' demanded some of the British troops.

'Germany and England of course, you twits.'

'What about Ireland, Scotland and Wales?'

'OK, it will be Germany v. Odds and Sods,' joked Field.

'Why not make it Germany v. Western Isles?' asked one imaginative trooper. 'That would include everybody.'

All agreed.

Representing Germany were Saxons for the most part because an entire football team from the region had enlisted together. This, of course, gave Fritz the advantage.

The players of the Western Isles were a motley crew; not only were they from different countries, but also you had R. J. Arbuthnot, an Eton old boy, and Jock O'Kane from the Glasgow Gorbals. O'Kane was a serious prospect who had been given a trial by Glasgow Celtic and even a Glasgow Rangers supporter present admitted that he was 'very handy with his feet'. War – or rather was it the truce? – was a great leveller. Scotland, or anywhere else, would never be quite the same again.

The Western Isles team was composed of three 2/Seaforth Highlanders – O'Kane being one of them. There were two from 2/Royal Dubliners, Moore and Clinch. Although both had fought in the Second Boer War, they were still only in their thirties and were fit men. Cochrane of the Dubliners was a fine player, but he was still not fully recovered from his encounter with the gigantic rat. This ruled him out. There were also two players from 1/East Lancashires and one footballer each from various other regiments.

Sergeant Major Field was an obvious choice for referee. While a policeman in London, he had served on the board of Arsenal Football Club for a time and was an ardent football fan. Strangely, he put a clock in his pocket as part of his preparation – he already wore a wristwatch.

Furlong said, 'He must want to be sure to be sure.'

The game proved a 'corker'. The ball swung from end to end and, although the Saxons had the more cohesion, the Western Isles played with great heart. Clinchie and Moore performed side by side in the defence and, urged on by cheerleader Barton ('Come on the Dubliners!') and sundry other buddies on the sideline, gave a huge performance. When a loud alarm clock went off in referee Field's pocket to signal half-time, the men cheered the initiative.

At the interval, the score stood at 1-1. Franz Reibensahm, a German international, had drilled home a cracking penalty, having been upended in the penalty area. Clinch, the perpetrator, swore it was no penalty and did it so loudly that referee Field threatened to send him off. The Western Isles' goal came from a melee in the goalmouth. A clearance from the German goalie hit Dai Jones, a Welshman serving in 1/Royal Warwicks, in the back of the head and rebounded over the line for a fluky score. It wasn't a glorious outcome, yet a rejoicing Jones ran outfield hugging all and sundry. To his mind, goals from cracking penalties or fluky headers came to the same thing. And history was on his side.

The second half proved no less intense and O'Kane didn't disappoint. After ten minutes, in true Scottish fashion, he glided like a ghost past three defenders and feinted a shot to the left corner of the net. The goalie – anticipating – dived in that direction, while a composed O'Kane side-footed the ball into the right corner: Western Isles 2 Germany 1.

By this time the crowd was wildly excited. The passing of the Germans was smoother, yet the spirit of the Westerners was carrying the day. Then, from nowhere, up pops Reibensahm again: Germany 2 Western Isles 2.

The Isles fans groaned. Just when they thought the momentum was with them disaster had struck, and Reibensahm was really showing his pedigree. The German fans were cock-a-hoop.

Time was running out and all the players were striving mightily. Then Klemm, the German outside left, who was having a quiet afternoon, unexpectedly drifted in from the side and sneaked a strategic header. Almost immediately the dire alarm clock rang out and, allowing a couple of minutes extra time, Field blew the final whistle. It ended Fritz 3 Tommy 2.

All the Germans lustily broke into *Die Wacht am Rhein*, while the Westerners good humouredly consoled themselves with *Pack Up Your Troubles*. As O'Kane said to Reibensahm: 'Okay Franz, you take the game, we'll be happy with the war.'

'Seems fair to me,' grinned the Saxon, and added, 'Wouldn't football be a better way of sorting out differences than war – make football not war.'

This remark stopped O'Kane in his tracks. He stood open-mouthed. It was true.

When the men reassembled after the game, O'Kane, captain of the Western Isles, sportingly proposed a toast to the winners, and Reibensahm one to the 'gallant losers'.

Then, amid great mirth, Furlong proposed a toast to the back of goal scorer Jones' head. And so the camaraderie continued until darkness was setting in and a sizeable, mellow Evening Star appeared in the sky. 'Reminds you of the star that guided the Magi,' remarked Sewald.

Looking to the morrow, a German officer said, 'Sadly I have to tell you that the British lines will be bombarded at 9.30 tomorrow morning. You would be wise to come over to our trenches for safety.'

'Thanks for the offer,' a British officer replied. 'Now if your people bomb our positions at 9.30, we are sure to bombard yours immediately afterwards. So you had better take refuge in ours also.'

'One more thing,' said the German officer, 'before renewing hostilities following our truce, we will first fire warning shots in the air.'

'And we will do the same,' the British officer assured them.

'I'm glad the rigorous Tom Evans isn't here at this point,' whispered Bentley to Barton.

'Me too. And the same goes for old Major-General Wilson. He'd have us all shot at dawn.'

They now fell silent. The young tenor of the night before once more began *Stille Nacht, Heilige Nacht* and all joined in. The Germans sang the words and the British hummed the solemn melody, which they were beginning to learn. *Silent Night* was not yet widely known in England or Ireland. When the last notes faded away, they shook hands, indeed many embraced and melted into the blue night. Laz, quite uncat-like, trotted along behind Barton. Some wondered if the unthinkable happenings of the last two days had merely been the stuff of dreams.

STAVE EIGHT

Eileen Dearest

On arriving back to his dugout Barton was still so excited that he felt an irresistible urge to write to his beloved Eileen Walsh. Besides, she had sent him a Christmas letter that needed answering, so he settled down to do so. Just then Lieutenant Leveridge, having strolled back in the bracing, luminous night, arrived.

'Hello, Barton. Not a comfortable place for penning your memoirs, and by candlelight.'

'No, sir, especially since there is so much to say.'

'Look, I have to go further along the trench on a little business. Why don't you use my quarters for a while?' said the officer, leading him down a few steps into what was a hovel really, but would be more suited to writing.

The men were growing to respect and like Leveridge more and more. He was a serious, somewhat reserved, young man but with a caring, generous side, as evidenced by his present offer.

Groping his way, the Lieutenant lit a storm lamp, which revealed the interior of his bolt hole with its touching efforts at domesticity: a gramophone with a huge horn, brazier, shelves, table and chair, tin containers, enamel plate and mug, kettle and teapot, a cape hanging on the earthen wall and a poster of two lovers, kissing in front of a tree with a heart carved on its bark. Barton sat at the bare wooden table and commenced to write.

Western Front
25 December 1914

Dearest Eileen,

I hope you have had a happy Christmas and thank you for your letter and the gift of a scarf and pullover. I know they are going to be invaluable for the remainder of the winter. As I write this, the frosty moon and stars look down on the frigid scene of an incredible revelation. Before I retire to rest, I must tell you about it. Could you believe that while you at home were enjoying your Christmas fare of goose, ham and plum pudding, we were out in No Man's Land eating, drinking, singing carols and playing football with our German 'enemies'? You find this hard to credit? I'm not surprised. I hardly believe it myself even though I was present.

But let me get to the point, Eileen. I want you to keep this letter which I, your fond lover, am writing on this momentous day, in case anything happens to me, which God forbid. What has transpired has been mould breaking – nothing quite like it has happened in history before. We have glimpsed a Promised Land where war will be no more, a unique moment in the long story of human beings that will stand as a challenge to remaining ages. Yes, let me say it again, the death knell of war has been sounded in Flanders this Yuletide. Paradoxically, given our dire situation, I have never lived through such a special Christmas. There hasn't been another like it since Bethlehem.

We found the German troops in Flanders to be human like ourselves, wanting this slaughter to end, so that we can all go home and be with those we love. Like most of us too, they are baffled as to what this strife is all about. That avalanche of propaganda regarding hatred between them and us is without the deep foundation it is supposed to have. It is nothing but the creation of monarchs, politicians and diplomats, greedy for money and power, yet out of touch with the sentiments, concerns, and indeed sufferings of ordinary people.

Just think about it, Eileen. Thousands are being needlessly slaughtered out here in the most deadly and inept war ever fought and, as with all wars, they will have to sit down at the finish and talk, so as to end it. Why can't they sit down right now and through dialogue and negotiation – hard though these may be – resolve their differences and save all those lives? That is the question being asked, not by the generals, but by the ordinary Fritz, Tommy and Paddy in Flanders this Christmas 1914. The question will endure until it is answered satisfactorily. Sooner or later this happening will lead to an era of peace. And such forces as exist will do so to save lives and preserve peace, rather than make war.

This is the world I crave for you, Eileen. When (I don't say 'if') we marry and have a child, it's the world I want for that child too.

You see I am sanguine about us getting married, despite your dad's opposition to my Protestantism. My supporting his life cause of Home Rule for Ireland by joining this conflict doesn't seem to have won him over. And it now looks as though Home Rule will no longer satisfy some ardent nationalists, who are seeking complete independence. So I suppose I am out on a limb. Concern for the men in my section keeps me motivated. The experience I had today, however, has given me such a warm feeling towards humanity, that I remain optimistic that your father may change his mind. Remember those words we loved to read as childhood sweethearts in our schoolbook years ago?

> And oh! it were a gallant deed
> To show before mankind,
> How every race and every creed
> Might be by love combined
> Might be combined, yet not forget
> The fountains whence they rose,
> As, filled with many a rivulet,
> The stately Shannon flows.

Eileen, I love you beyond all telling. I look forward to the days when we will be able to stroll along the banks of the Avonree once more. Meanwhile, stay well and God bless you. I'll close now and go to rest, wearied by the celebrations and stimulation of this never to be forgotten Christmas.

Yours ever,

Lenny xxx

As he perused the letter he had just written, he marvelled at Thomas Davis' poem and his openness to difference as far back as the 1840s. And, like himself, he was a Protestant. Leveridge returned in the midst of this musing.

Seeing that Barton was still present, he realised that it was the opportunity he had been waiting for. 'Cup of tea, Barton?'

'Yes please, sir.'

'Remember your enigmatic remark about coming to Flanders in search of a bride?'

'I do.'

'Would you like to solve the enigma?'

'Certainly.'

So, as they gently sipped their tea, Barton revealed his travails in love to his Commanding Officer. When he had finished, Leveridge said, 'You are a calm, patient man, Barton. No lover of conflict. I know that somehow you'll win through in the end.'

STAVE NINE

The Truce Recedes

At 9 a.m. on St Stephen's Day 1914, Sergeant Clinch rallied his men. 'The German bombardment of our positions is due to begin in thirty minutes. Better get over to the shelter of the "enemy" trenches now.' As he uttered the word 'enemy', he made inverted commas in the air with his fingers. Together with other troops of the 2/Royal Dublin Fusiliers, they moved to the German redoubts.

Promptly, at 9.30 a.m. the German bombardment of the British positions began, as the German participants in the truce had predicted. The Allies watched the mayhem from the safety of the 'enemy' trenches. The British artillery duly responded and the Germans found shelter in the Allied dugouts.

Shots were later fired by both sides and the truce was officially over. Orders had come from the opposing HQs to intensify hostilities. It was only over in a sense though, because, as promised, the shots were fired over the heads of opposing troops. They had also undertaken to give adequate warning when lethal fire was about to begin. Several thousand rounds of ammunition ended up being discharged harmlessly towards the stars.

News of the truce, which had occurred sporadically across two-thirds of the British line, had reached the Allied HQ at St Omer and the Generals, particularly Smith-Dorrien, were spitting blood. Orders came to all officers forbidding fraternisation with the enemy and threatening court martial and dire consequences for those who engaged in such reprehensible behaviour.

'There's nothing the Generals can do beyond huffing and puffing,' said Clinch to his section of 'B' Company, 'If all the troops involved were to be court-martialled and shot, you'd destroy the British Expeditionary Force.'

What the Generals did was turn a discreet blind eye to, and play down, the events. They also resolved to make sure that a Christmas truce would never again occur while the conflict lasted.

The Generals' position had a degree of support among the

men. Some of the troops were quite dismayed by the truce, seeing it as a clear case of collaboration with the enemy.

Even 'B' Company of the Dubliners had its dissident. While the men were celebrating in No Man's Land, the rigorous Thomas Evans had found a Captain who gave a ready ear to the charge of treason against them and guaranteed him that, however difficult it might be, he would see to it that the message reached the highest echelons. The result was that the Generals had to engage in sound and fury, although in the end it signified nothing.

Evans was not alone in the British ranks. Major A. J. C. Duckworth from the St Omer HQ while 'admonishing' Leveridge said, 'There were shining examples of soldiers who adamantly refused to be part of any treasonous truce. That was true of the Boche too. For many of them it was business as usual on Christmas Day, which should have called for high alertness on our part.'

'With respect, sir, aren't the words 'treason' and 'treachery' that are being bandied about to describe a mutually agreed cessation of hostilities something of a gross exaggeration? What about the understanding between ourselves and the enemy to have a breakfast truce each day to give the men a chance to eat and clean up?' Leveridge argued.

'Confound it man, those aren't truces. They're totally different.'

'How?'

'It's obvious.'

'Is it really?

'Listen, Captain –'

'Lieutenant, sir.'

'All the more reason why you should listen. Still wet behind the ears. Just out of university. Why didn't you consult HQ?'

'On Christmas Eve? It was all done spontaneously by the men – a breather after months of hell. We had to do the best we could on the spot. Just as we often have to do in the heat of battle. There are times when we can hardly communicate along the front line with those nearest to us, never mind St Omer. You know well, sir, that communications are a problem.'

'Others did their patriotic duty,' Duckworth continued relentlessly. 'Towards the southern end of the line, 2/Grenadier Guards were having a torrid time with the Boche, while your men were carousing. At daybreak on the 25th some Huns put their heads above the trenches and shouted "Merry Christmas!" After the hard time they got on the previous day, the Guards were in no mood for camaraderie. They fired on them. And I tell you, that got their heads down quickly. Intense sniper fire between them continued all day.'

'A sad way to spend Christmas Day.'

'Those brave Guards didn't think so. There was a similar rebuff in the northern sector of the 3rd Division. Captain Billy Congreve gave strict orders that there was to be no truce. There were rumours that the Boche were going to try and arrange one. They actually came towards the British singing. Congreve ordered his men to fire on them declaring, "That's the only truce they deserve!" I could go on giving you examples, but I think that's quite enough.'

'Indeed, sir. Thank you.'

'You know a trooper in a letter, referring to a speech by Prime Minister Asquith, wrote that it was alright for him to make grandiose statements about not sheathing the sword until the war was won. That was fine, he opined, for people safe back in England but, if you were in Flanders it was hard to keep on hating poor sods who were suffering the same deprivations as yourself. This is sentimental nonsense. Undermines and weakens our position. Did you ever hear anything as insane as that, Leveridge?'

'Almost everything I've heard was more insane than that.'

Either Duckworth's brain failed to process this, or, in his sense of outrage, he wasn't listening anyway – probably the latter. 'Stop hating! What next? Fraternities between enemy forces?' he ranted. 'What piffle!'

'Indeed, sir. There's no telling where it will all end.'

'Well, Lieutenant, it's all got to end right now. Go back to your 2/Dubliners and make sure it does, or the Generals of the High Command will have your guts for garters.'

'Good day, Major. I hope you had a good Christmas.'

'Capital meal, old chap, and – Confound it! What's that got to do with you?'

Leveridge returned to the trenches, entered his 'quarters', poured himself a Glenfiddich and lit a cigar – the remains of Yuletide. He didn't even bother to burden the men with the injunctions of Major A. J. C. Duckworth. Having come to Flanders on a wave of what he now saw as naïve patriotism, he was growing more disillusioned day by day with this war.

As for the Christmas truce, rather than cease abruptly, it faded away like the Cheshire Cat in *Alice in Wonderland*. There was a reluctance among many of the troops to fire on the men they had befriended over Yuletide, so they were quietly transferred to other locations. In the case of the fading Cheshire Cat, eventually all that was left was the smile. But there's the rub, mused Leveridge. The smile remained forever. So, too, will the memory and challenge of the truce.

STAVE TEN

Known Only to God

On a summer's evening in the early 1950s, Lenny Barton was walking down Bridge Street in Ballybeg, County Kilkenny when he noticed a group of curious onlookers gathered around something on the road. Among them were many noisy urchins who were clearly having a hilarious time. He went to see what was happening. A drunken man was squatting on all fours furiously beating the road with one of his shoes. He pushed through the crowd to reach him.

'Come on home, Michael. You'll be alright.'

Michael Cochrane looked at him vacantly for a moment. Then pleaded, 'Lenny, help me!'

'Put on your shoe and come with me. You're safe now. They can't harm you.'

He put on his shoe and Lenny helped him to his feet, linked him by the arm and led him away. He went meekly. As he did so a man in the midst of the amused children asked, 'What ails the fellow? What was he up to?'

'Killing rats,' Lenny answered shortly. What was the point of trying to explain the hell that Michael and all the other ex-soldiers of the Great War had been through? And here they were now, strangers in their own land. Men who were away earning the Saxon shilling while patriotic Irishmen were fighting for Irish independence.

Lenny put Michael in his car and drove him home.

***

'Thanks a lot, Lenny, for coming to my aid,' said Michael when next they met. 'I'd had a few drinks and you know it only takes a little to set me off.'

'It's the least I could do for an old companion in 'B' Company.'

'It's hard to think that there are only three survivors of our section. And two of us are from this little town.'

'Michael,' said Lenny gravely, 'no one survived the Great War intact. In one way or another we were all scarred by it. There are only victims.'

'Yeah, it's true. But it's hard to take when people don't want to know us. We are the forgotten ones. It's best not to talk about it.'

Lenny put a comforting arm round Michael's shoulder and asked, 'How are Bridie and the family?'

'Okay, thank God. Our army pension is small, but isn't it well to have it? Work is on and off. The economy is shattered. So many people leaving the country. It's sad. You could fire a cannonball the length of Green Street and you wouldn't hit a soul.'

***

Following his encounter with Michael, Lenny reflected on his own life trajectory. Like Michael, he had survived the war but not without travail. He recalled the Christmas truce of 1914. There were a lot of regulars present for that, and of those only one in ten outlasted the lengthy, mindless slaughter. With the rest of 'B' Company he went over the top at the Somme in 1916. They were barely out of the trench when Sean Furlong crumpled to the ground. Lenny had run to his side and whispered a prayer in his ear.

'Thanks,' Sean muttered and then looked at the blood cascading from his chest. With a faint smile, he spoke weakly, 'Would that this were for Ireland! I joined for adventure, Lenny. Not a great reason was it?'

'Sean, you kept all our hearts up. You were the staff of your pals.'

'Was I?' he asked with a look of surprise. His head then lolled to one side and the happy warrior was gone.

With a tear crawling down his cheek Lenny recalled saying, 'You most definitely were', and then having to hurry off to rejoin the ranks, many of whom were marching like lemmings to their deaths.

That marching was suicidal. They were being cut to pieces by machine-gun and mortar fire. They thought the Germans had been shelled out of existence by the fierce bombardment that had preceded the attack, but not so. When the bombardment stopped, they ran out of their deep, strong bunkers and commenced scything down the masses marching towards their positions. Even the 'fat boys' weighing ninety kilos hadn't wreaked too much damage on their defences, because there weren't enough of them.

The Allied forces had been told that orderly marching was best, since many of them were raw recruits and training them to charge headlong without causing utter confusion would take too much time. Besides, they didn't expect to find many survivors of the artillery barrage. The Germans couldn't believe their luck. It was a turkey shoot. The casualties on the first day were so numerous that the Germans eased off at midday and ceased firing altogether in the afternoon to give the British a chance to attend to the dead and wounded. By that time there were 60,000 casualties, 20,000 of them fatal.

Lenny had been one of them. He was wounded in the chest and in a hailstorm of lead and steel crawled into a shell hole and lay there in agony.

In the evening, when the shooting had died down, a German soldier with fixed bayonet stood on the side of his shell hole. With horror Lenny had realised what he was about to do. Just as the trooper was going to run him through, an officer appeared from nowhere and with his own gun smacked the weapon upward. The soldier gave him a surprised look. 'Take this man prisoner and bring him to a dressing station.' It was Captain Rolf Sewald; he gave the wounded man a quiet nod of recognition. The soldier did as commanded.

At the station, they found that the wound, though serious, was not fatal. And they found something else. A cross he was wearing had a deep dent where a bullet had glanced off it. It had saved his life.

'Where did you get that cross?' asked the doctor who treated him.

'From Eileen, my sweetheart.'

'Well you can thank Eileen. She saved your life. Keep the cross as a souvenir.'

At first Lenny had spent some time at a hospital in Valenciennes, which proved a good place with kind doctors and nurses. Sewald probably helped to get him there, because he soon received a note from the Captain wishing him well. Obviously it had come from the front because it was smudged with mud. After two months, he was transferred to Limberg Prisoner of War Camp. The prisoners there were treated well enough but, as the war edged towards a close, he would probably have starved if it weren't for the parcels that came from the Red Cross. At that point, even the German people were starving.

Lenny was demobbed in the summer of 1919 and, although national affairs in Ireland were reaching boiling point, he spent weeks of bliss, mostly in the arms of Eileen. It was a good summer and they went for long walks by the Avonree, swam in its limpid water – the trout gambolling about in it were clearly visible – and talked endlessly.

After some weeks, Lenny decided it was time to confront the daunting Jack Walsh once more on the possibility of marriage to his daughter. Eileen was not too hopeful but felt it was worth a try.

In early September he called at the Walsh farm.

'Come in, Lenny,' said Jack, 'you're most welcome. As I already told you, it's great to have you back home with us safe and sound.'

'Thank you, Jack, I've come to have a word with you.'

'In that case come into the parlour here. Maura!', he called out to his wife, 'Lenny's here.'

She came to greet him and then said, 'Sit in there with Jack and I'll bring you a cup of tea.'

'And how are you settling back into civilian life, Lenny?'

'Fine, Jack. It's quite a change.'

'I can imagine.'

'How's the farm going?'

'I haven't got involved yet, but the brother, James, has the hay saved and is now preparing to tackle the corn.'

'The weather has been good, thank God.'

They continued chatting amiably for a while. Lenny was sure Jack knew why he was there, but he wanted to give Maura a chance to serve the tea before raising the issue. She soon entered carrying a tray laden with the tea things and mouth-watering scones, country butter and strawberry jam.

'God, Maura, you have enough to feed an army here,' exclaimed Lenny.

'Enjoy,' urged Maura, and discreetly withdrew.

They ate in silence for some moments.

'Jack, I'm sure you know why I'm here. I'm asking for Eileen's hand in marriage.'

'Lenny, I deeply admire how you joined the army to fight for Home Rule and the freedom of small nations, as John Redmond requested. I also appreciate you as a man of integrity and I know that your family were always good to my people.'

'Thanks.'

'Regarding marriage with Eileen, we've been over this ground before. It isn't that I don't want to give consent, it's just that I can't. It's the difference in religions.'

'Eileen and I are both Christians.'

'But you're Protestant and she's Catholic.'

'I'm perfectly sincere about what I believe in,' blurted Lenny.

'I know you are, but in my view also quite mistaken.'

'Meaning?'

'Lenny, a king can't start a religion. Only God can do that.'

'Eileen and I love each other to distraction and, in the end, only love matters.'

'Maybe you're right. Maybe things will be different in the future, although I don't see how. If you were to turn, that would change everything. But you are firm in your belief and I cling to mine. Neither of us can change. It's a bridge too far for me.'

Seeing how adamant Jack was, Lenny knew that any further talk would be futile, so, devastated, he took his leave.

Jack grasped his hand, shook it and said, 'Sorry.'

Lenny went to tell Eileen what had transpired. She was equally distressed but, though she had allowed herself to hope, she was not surprised at the outcome.

What Lenny or Eileen didn't know was that an event back in 1916 had not helped their cause. Evans was wounded at the Somme and, as a result, was given a short furlough in Ireland. Unfortunately, while he was awaiting the permission to go home for his break, Michael Cochrane had innocently told him of Lenny's great love for Eileen and of their desire to marry.

'Is Eileen also a Protestant?' enquired Evans.

'No, she's Catholic.'

'Marriage is not a good idea, then.' Evans was adamant. The possibility seemed to upset his rigorous religious mindset inordinately and had dire consequences.

While on furlough in Dublin, he travelled to visit a sister in Clonmel, County Tipperary. When booking the trip, he found that his bus passed through Ballybeg – the hometown of Barton. Whether it was a matter of conscience, or brooding resentment towards Lenny, he took the trouble to stop there and seek out Jack Walsh. He strove to impress upon Jack that a marriage between Barton and Eileen was not a good idea – as if he needed persuading. For good measure he had visited the Parish Priest and told him that Lenny was not a fit subject for marriage to Eileen; a statement that could have meant anything. Anyway, the priest was ambivalent on the subject of mixed marriages. Those interventions were far from helpful – to put it mildly.

Long afterwards, Lenny found out about the visit and wondered what, in addition to his obviously narrow-minded religiosity, might have driven his nemesis to such lengths. He thought of a saying that a Lancashire trooper at the front used repeatedly: 'There's nowt as strange as folks.' How true. Maybe Evans' own rebuffs in love explained the compulsive behaviour? Or was it an inability to relate at all? He hadn't excelled in relating to his companions at the front. Indeed it could have been, as often happens, a case of unacknowledged jealousy towards Barton. Lenny was a man who was beloved, not only by his fiancée, but by people generally. For one human being to plumb the depths of another's heart is not possible. Quite frankly, he was an enigma for Lenny, a problem to which there was no solution.

But, within a few years of returning from the war, things were about to change dramatically for Lenny. Eileen contracted a most virulent form of tuberculosis, the type called galloping consumption – the curse of the Irish. He was utterly distraught and rarely left her side at Peamount Hospital in Dublin. Though devastated, he tried to keep the best side out for her sake.

While joking together one day, Eileen teased him about all the nice girls he must have met in France, where they are so beautiful and chic.

'Oh yes,' he retorted. 'There was one in particular.'

'*And who was she*?' demanded Eileen.

'She was known as Mademoiselle from Armentières.'

'Was she now? And very well known by the sound of it.'

'Yes, hugely popular.'

In the tragic time that remained, the Mademoiselle often made for a light moment.

The hospital Chaplain, Fr Quigley, often came to see Eileen. They chatted with him, but the atmosphere was strained. He too thought mixed marriages were a bad idea.

'While in love, the couple gloss over the problems that lie in wait,' he said. 'When children come along, they find the difference in religion does matter. What in the time of courtship seemed a molehill, then becomes a mountain. This often leads to a break-up.'

To change the subject Lenny told him about Fr Ryan the RC Chaplain in the war: a fearless man, beloved of Protestant Ulstermen and Catholic southerners alike, blown to pieces at Passchendaele.

As Fr Quigley went to continue his visitation of the patients, he thought of how radiant Eileen looked, and yet there was that heightened brightness in the eyes that presages the end through tuberculosis. A saying common among the people came to mind: 'Consumption has no pity on blue eyes or golden hair.'

Next day, Lenny appeared with a bottle of champagne and some canapés.

'What's this in aid of?'

'Eileen, no matter what anybody says, I think that before God we are married. And I want to assure you that you will be the only love of my life.'

She was silent for a long time and tears glistened in her eyes, when she replied, 'Darling, you don't have to make any foolish promises. I know our love has been fulfilling for both of us, but you don't have to rule out finding love again because of me.'

'Are you listening, Eileen? No one can or will take your place – it's not a promise, it's a vow.' And he sealed it with a kiss, as both of them wept profusely, yet happily.

Six weeks later Eileen died. The year was 1923.

***

Lenny lived on into the 1960s farming quietly. On a glorious July day in 1932, he returned from haymaking and saw a man leaving the premises. Thinking he looked familiar, Lenny hurried after him. Indeed it was he. 'Hello, Brian, how are you?' It was Moorie, third survivor of the old section of 'B' Company, looking somewhat the worse for wear.

'Is it Lenny?'

'It is.'

'The lady inside –'

'My sister Hyacinth.'

'Gave me a nice sandwich and a cup of tea. Thanks.'

'Come back and join us for our evening meal. I'm delighted to see you after all these years.'

'I … I can't –'

'I'll not take no for an answer.' And he led Brian inside and introduced him properly to Hyacinth.

Lenny knew much of Brian's turbulent story, but not all. After news of the Easter Rising came in 1916, he was so upset by the execution of the leaders that he refused to fight anymore for the Crown. To make matters worse, a cousin of his on the nationalist side was killed in the rebellion. His decision put the military authorities in a quandary. He had been decorated twice for bravery during the Boer War, famously at the Siege of Mafeking. This made it difficult to have him court-martialled and shot for cowardice. Instead they sent him to a facility for psychological assessment in England and eased him out of the army.

'What are you up to these times, Brian?' Lenny enquired as they were having a drink after the evening meal.

'I winter in the Liberties, but I get out of Dublin from May to September and go walkabout. I go from farm to farm and am given food; do a little work here and there, sleep in barns or wherever. In short I have become a travelling man – a man of the roads.'

'You enjoy it?'

'After all the marching I done in the South African veldt, in France and Flanders, I just can't stop going. I can't seem to kick the habit. I'm restless. Maybe I'm just passing through a phrase or something.'

Lenny smiled, remembering Brian's near misses with words.

'You know that Clinchie was killed at Whitesheet?' he shot out of the blue.

'Yes.'

'My old buddy Clinchie. We went through the Boer War together and almost two years of the Great War. We always looked out for each other. If I had been with him there on Messines Ridge in 1917, he might still be alive. It haunts me still.'

'If I knew Sergeant Clinch, he wouldn't want you to punish yourself over that.'

'Do you really think so?' he asked earnestly while blowing his nose in a grubby handkerchief.

'I really do.'

And so the conversation between these two old comrades continued late into the night.

Next day Lenny bade him goodbye at the gate, saying, 'Brian, there's always a welcome for you in this house and never forget that. It's an order.'

The old hero of Mafeking snapped to attention and shouted, 'Yes, sir!'

***

Over the years Lenny had learned about the fate of other war-time colleagues. He enquired about his friend and saviour Captain Rolf Sewald through the good offices of the German Embassy in Dublin. At 3.10 p.m. on 7 June 1917, the 3rd Battle of Messines was launched. It began with the detonation of nineteen massive mines containing one million pounds of explosives. It was the loudest sound made in history; the greatest man-made explosion the world had ever seen. The noise was heard as far away as London. In an instant, entire German companies were snuffed out and Sewald, who was in a bunker at the summit of Messines Ridge, was simply vaporised with hundreds of others. He and Lenny would never meet again as they had hoped to do.

As the malignant figure of Adolf Hitler came to dominate the world stage during the 1930s and 40s, Lenny often reflected bitterly on how he seemed to negate the sacrifices of his comrades. Of Ned Stack, quiet George Belford and Percy Bentley who, like Sean

Furlong, had fallen by the Somme. And of course Cristopher Clinch, James McGovern, Thomas Evans and Edward McHugh, who gave their lives on the slopes of Messines Ridge. Within a course of little more than twenty years, it had to be done all over again.

Lieutenant Patrick Leveridge was the unluckiest of all. He was killed by artillery fire at 10.45 a.m. on 11 November 1918 – fifteen minutes before the Armistice! What stupid people, Barton often wondered, were so gung-ho that they were still giving hell to those they dismissed as the Boche with only minutes to go to the end of the Great War that had already cost 21 million lives, inflicting needless sorrow on loved ones back home. Madness. Patrick Leveridge deserved better than a lonely grave in Flanders.

Lenny had found hope in the fact that men of the 16th Irish Division – mostly Catholic southerners – and the 36th Ulster Division – largely Protestant – advanced up Messines Ridge together and, indeed, died and were buried side by side. He wondered how this sat with the narrow-minded Thomas Evans who had done him harm and later did some more to others. He had mixed feelings towards this complicated, dour man. However, it was hard to quarrel with someone who had gone up the hill and given his life for whatever he believed in. In a war where for years progress was measured in yards, those Irishmen advanced seven kilometres in one day to take Wytschaete. A heroic feat.

As for those comrades of his section who died at the Somme or Messines Ridge, no trace was ever found – the lot of countless thousands in the Great War. Even the dead Sean Furlong was obliterated by subsequent shellfire. Like the identities of so many who lie in Flanders beneath the serried ranks of gleaming Allied gravestones and dark German crosses, their whereabouts are known only to God.

Reminiscing on the fate of the principal participants in the Christmas truce of 1914 had been sweet sorrow for Lenny Barton and Michael Cochrane over the decades. Michael outlived Lenny by a few years – he was the last to go. Lenny lived out his years in Ballybeg. The people referred to him as 'a proper gentleman' and there is no greater accolade. When a neighbour died, Catholic or

Protestant, he was always at the funeral in his usual position, halfway up the church.

He himself passed away in 1963 and the Protestant pastor was amazed at the crowd – overwhelmingly Catholic – that filled the church to capacity and overflowed into the grounds outside. The times were changing. Lenny Barton, who had long ago crossed No Man's Land, had at last been met halfway by his 'adversaries', coming from the other side. And he had kept the vow made to Eileen forty years before.

STAVE ELEVEN

God's Other Creatures

Not only was Lenny Barton interested in the fate of humans, he also thought of God's other creatures – especially Laz. He had not seen the cat since he had been wounded and taken prisoner at the Somme. But Michael Cochrane had news which he'd shared with Lenny on being demobbed.

According to Michael, Laz was out of sorts for quite a while after the Somme. 'You know, Lenny, I think he was pining for you.'

'Hardly, Michael, cats are independent creatures. They attach themselves to the person who will give them food. It's a matter of self-interest.'

'You'd have to be a cat yourself to be sure of that.'

'Difficult to achieve, Michael.'

'The point is that Laz really pined for you. He seemed to know of our friendship and kept on mewing at me and looking into my eyes as if he wanted to say, "Where's Lenny?" I'm convinced he was missing you. If it was food he wanted, he could have gone to that old sweat Clinchie; that gourmet always managed to have something in his knapsack, even when the rest of us were on the verge of starvation.'

'You're right. Clinchie was never without a crust; 'twas ingen - ious how he got his hands on food.'

'Time is a great healer, as they say, and Laz recovered at last and just got on with his usual routine of befriending the Germans, ourselves and the French as he begged for food. ''Twas a sad day that he had rubbings with the French though.'

'Why?'

'Remember Evans?'

'Rather.'

'For some unknown reason he got his knife in poor old Laz. You may remember his suspicious remark about the comings and goings of the cat between the lines at that great Christmas dinner in 1914. Once Laz started 'bumming' around among the French,

Evans sought out the Captain who was his conduit to the higher ranks. They in turn warned the French about this 'dangerous' feline, which put them on the alert. As luck would have it, one day Laz wandered back from the German lines and intelligence found a note in his collar: 'What is the name of your regiment?' was the question.

'Sounds innocuous enough. Just trying to make contact. The regiment you are faced with hardly matters. They all fought just as fiercely.'

'There is even a question as to whether the Germans put the note there at all. However, whoever put it there, the reaction was unbelievable. There was an uproar. Laz was tried by a French military tribunal, found guilty of treason and sentenced to be executed.'

'You're joking surely.'

'I wish I was, Lenny.'

'But this is the stuff of comic opera.'

'Yes, but there was nothing funny about his death.'

Lenny was wide-eyed with incredulity. 'You mean … you mean they actually went through with it?'

'Sadly, yes. The firing squad was in position. Laz was brought out. The officer in command decided there was no need to tie the animal to the stake of execution. He was placed in front of it and stood there purring and unsuspecting in the slanting sun.'

'This has to be a wind-up,' blurted Lenny.

'Ready! Aim! – When Laz heard orders being barked and rifles pointed, awful memory told him what to expect. He dashed towards some nearby bushes. *Fire!* This time he didn't make it.'

Lenny stood dumbfounded for some minutes and then asked, 'What, Michael, could possibly have been the meaning of that charade?'

'Look, in terms of life, it was only an ould cat –'

'Only an ould cat? 'Twas one of God's creatures who was the centre of his own universe and in his environment had skills superior to those of any human. What right had they to snuff his life out?'

'You know what I think, Lenny. The French troops, many of them humble peasants torn from their farms, were really fed up and on the verge of mutiny. They even had to bring in the popular Marshal Pétain to hold things together. Those in command made an example of the cat. They were saying, "This is what is going to happen to you if there's any trouble." Otherwise the whole exercise would have been totally ridiculous and the ones who did it would have gone down in history as complete fools.'

'You are a cunning fellow, Michael Cochrane, and I think you have a point. But it spelled the end for poor Laz.'

'I'll tell you something else, Lenny, the French authorities should put right a terrible injustice and clear the cat's name.'

Did it really spell the end for Laz though? There lived in Ballybeg a man called Paddy Hogan, who developed a keen interest in the Great War, including the Christmas truce. In his youth, he would have known Lenny and Michael. While visiting Flanders in later years, he took a photograph of the field near Ploegsteert Wood, where the truce took place.

'It was difficult to take,' he explained to Michael Cochrane's son, Martin, 'because it was completely covered with a tall crop of green-stalked maize.'

'How did you manage? Did you hire a helicopter?' asked Martin.

'That wasn't within the pocket of a poor photographer. I did the best I could by photographing it from the side.'

'Hardly satisfactory, Paddy.'

'Well, at least I got a record of the sacred spot.'

'What's that cat doing in the photo?'

'Good question. I got a surprise when I developed this picture, because I didn't remember seeing that cat when I took it.'

'That's strange.'

'More strange than you may realise.'

'How come, Paddy?'

'Look at this cat. It has a fetching grey coat crossed with tiger-ish black stripes. Believe it or not, there is a cat named Laz, who figures in the story of the Christmas truce, and answers to that description.'

'So?'

'Are we looking at a cat who is living out one of his remaining nine lives, or is this the Ghost Cat of Flanders? Think about it.'

***

While all this was happening to Laz, Cher Ami was making his own news.

The Americans entered the war in its latter stages, much to the relief of the hard-pressed Allies. On 3 October 1918, Major Charles Whittlesey found himself and his 77th US Infantry Division of more than 500 men in a desperate situation. They were a lost battalion, out of sight of their own men. And they were trapped in a small depression on the side of a hill in the Argonne Forest area of France, surrounded by the Germans and being cruelly bombarded by them. By 4 October most of them had been slaughtered – only 200 remained. To add to their woes, they were also being shelled and killed by friendly fire from their own artillery.

'Friendly fire!' exclaimed one baffled trooper, 'Jeez, whoever describes it like that ain't foolin' nobody only themselves.'

In desperation, Major Whittlesey penned a message to the Commanding Officer of 308 Infantry:

We are along the road parallel 276.4
Our own artillery is dropping a barrage directly on us.
For heavens sake stop it.

Whittlesey
Major 308

All lines of communication were down. The only hope of sending the message was by carrier pigeon. He sent for the pigeon handler, Omer Richards, who hurriedly came with a coop. When he opened it, there were only two birds remaining.

'Is that all there is?' asked the Major.

'Afraid so,' answered Omer. 'The Germans know only too well what their work is and cut them out of the skies with sniper fire.'

Richards chose the more likely of the two. Just then there was a huge explosion nearby that showered Whittlesey and those around him with debris. The startled bird escaped from the hands of the handler. He lunged after it crying, 'Come back you stupid pigeon!' To no avail. All eyes looked after him in despair as he rapidly flew through the aftermath of the explosion.

At the bottom of the coop was the last remaining bird. 'Last chance saloon,' uttered the Major hopelessly and with reason.

Standing there was a scrawny black and grey chequered pigeon. Those around looked at him without much hope, because he was none too robust. It was Cher Ami.

With head still buzzing from the explosion, Richards, gritting his teeth, fastened the little aluminium tube containing the message to the leg of the pigeon. He then launched Cher Ami into a sky bristling with scrap and steel. The bird made three circles, didn't like what he saw and landed petrified on a bedraggled tree.

Richards threw a stick and shouted, 'Get goin' you cowardly bum!' Seeing their last hope disappearing, others also threw sticks and stones in an effort to dislodge him. But budge he would not.

Then, throwing caution to the wind, Richards dashed down the slope amid shot and shell and started shimmying up the tree as bullets ripped off the bark around his hands.

He shook the tree and yelled at the bird. No joy. He climbed higher and shook the branch the pigeon was sitting on. That did it. Amid cheers drowned out by explosions he took off. Richards jumped down from the tree and scrambled back up the incline to safety.

Then disaster struck. A shell exploded just below the bird killing five men and the pigeon fluttered to the ground.

The men groaned in desolation. Their only hope was gone. 'Lord, I want to see Eleanor and the kids again,' pleaded one private, without ever expecting to do so.

After a long silence among the troops, broken only by the occasional sob, a voice cried out, 'Look, the pigeon!' All heads turned towards Cher Ami. Phoenix-like he had spread his wings and started to rise. Higher and higher he soared. As they crouched in shell holes, the men could scarcely breathe as they watched the unbearable drama.

Again the sky was alive with bullets. But even the Germans had been taken unawares by what was happening. This time Cher Ami got away.

Joy among the men was unconfined. From their sheltered positions, they waved their helmets, wept, laughed and rent the heavens with their cheers. With dimmed eyes, Major Whittlesey watched the departing hero.

Astonishingly, Cher Ami flew twenty-five miles in as many minutes to deliver his message.

Lieutenant Pelham Bissell and Corporal George Gault were the signalmen on duty when the buzzer sounded to announce that a carrier pigeon had arrived at the loft. Gault hurried over to collect the communication. There he saw Cher Ami, listing to one side with a wound in his chest. When he reached in to retrieve him, the stricken creature collapsed completely. He then saw that he was bleeding profusely from the chest wound, had lost an eye, and the tube bearing the dire tidings was scarcely hanging by the torn tendons of a missing leg. This poor little guy has gone through hell to get his message here, thought Gault. He was once told that carrier pigeons sometimes fly on their spirit. It was true. On reading the communication, he rushed to pass on the information to the Commanding Officer of 308 Infantry. Then, just as speedily, he phoned the vet to come and save the gravely wounded hero.

Several days later, Cher Ami was comfortably nestled in his coop and still recovering from his wounds. The signalmen had treated him with tenderness, even fashioning a tiny wooden leg for him, so that he could get about. Two soldiers had entered the loft and were in the middle of a conversation.

'You say they formally court-martialled and tried the cat?'
'Exactly.'
'You have to be joking.'
'I know it sounds ridiculous, but that was how it was.'
'Good God, those French have to be crazy.'
'He was found guilty –'
(Cher Ami held his breath)
'and executed next day at dawn.'
'Have they gone stark, raving mad?'
'No, I'm sure they had a good reason.'
His companion looked at him in astonishment.
The other paused dramatically before adding, 'If you can think of it, let me know!'
'I certainly – Hey, look at Cher Ami.'
'What's the matter?'
'There's water streaming from that good eye of his.'

'Hi, old boy! You do look in bad shape. Better get the vet. Don't want him to lose that other eye.'

'I think he's weeping.'

'Nonsense, pigeons don't weep.'

Oh yes we do ... yes we do.

'Mind you, he's nothing to weep about. There isn't a bird that flies that wouldn't love to be standing in his shoes – so to speak.'

'You mean "shoe". Don't forget he's missing one of his pins.'

It was with a heavy heart that the brave bird was taken to the United States soon after. He was no longer a hero merely to the 77th Infantry Division but to the whole army and every American citizen. The French awarded him the Croix de Guerre for his exploits and General John J. Pershing 'a silver medal'. After all, he had saved the lives of 200 soldiers. He would gladly have exchanged both awards for the exoneration of Laz. To his mind, he was the true hero – a champion of reconciliation and peace.

On 13 June 1919, not even a year after he had completed his service with the Army Signal Corps, Cher Ami died of his many war wounds. The little hero is preserved in the Smithsonian Institution, Washington DC. Beside him is the Croix de Guerre with palm branch awarded by France. There he stands, on one leg, an inspiration to generations of Americans and, indeed, to all the peoples of the world.

STAVE TWELVE

Finale

The Walsh family cherished Lenny's historic letter from the trenches to Eileen for Christmas 1914. In it a precious memory was preserved, a moment in history when the world got a glimpse of a possible era of lasting peace. It would be a new age in which adversaries would resolve their differences through reason, dialogue and experiencing one another's common humanity. It would be a time for people to boldly cross No Man's Land and bridge divides. All who saw the letter felt a deep debt of gratitude to its author, as indeed they felt for the deeds of all the actors, human and other, in that amazing Yuletide drama of long ago. God bless them every one.